SHE NEVER KNEW

SHE NEVER KNEW

A Doc Wakefield Mystery

DEB NICHOLSON

gatekeeper press

Columbus, Ohio

She Never Knew: A Doc Wakefield Mystery

Published by Gatekeeper Press
3971 Hoover Rd. Suite 77
Columbus, OH 43123-2839
www.GatekeeperPress.com

ISBN: 9781619848382
eISBN: 9781619848399

Printed in the United States of America

"You are the captain of your ship.
You make your own luck."

—Dr. William R. Huff

CONTENTS

CHAPTER 1

Oakwood, NJ 9:15 AM

*D*AMN, DAMN, *DAMN! I don't want to face that woman.*
I don't want to deal with her.
That's all the rage that I could muster as I stood on the sidewalk facing the perfect home of Madison Chambers. Perfect tree tree-lined street, perfect house, perfect grass, and perfect freaking flowers! No peeling paint, weeds, dandelions or dog poop on the lawn like normal people have. Oh no! Not Madison—she was, well, PERFECT!

I had grown up with her. We didn't notice one another in grade school or middle school. The horror came in high school just as we were battling the tsunami of hormones and college applications. Madison had emerged from the storm like a graceful butterfly leaving the chrysalis. By contrast, I emerged like some mess that flies out of the blender when you forget to put the lid on tightly. She was lovely. Long red hair, naturally straight teeth, luminous skin and a knack for manipulating people without them either knowing or caring about it. She wasn't the sharpest pencil in the box, but she always managed to get ahead and get exactly what she wanted. She was one of the popular girls. The cheerleading squad went out of their way to recruit her, boys fell over themselves to date her, and nerds like me feared her.

I was about the same build as Madison but was shy and awkward, with unimpressive limp blonde hair, braces on my teeth and glasses. Whenever an important occasion came up, so did a new crop of zits—right across my forehead and nose. My only saving features were an IQ of 159 paired with an unusual eidetic memory. So, I was a genius with a gift for remembering, in vivid detail, images, sounds and words. Eidetic memory is not tied to intelligence—I just happened to get both. The downside was that I was socially awkward and considered to be borderline creepy by most of my peers. I was far from a hot commodity on the dating market.

I slithered along the high school hallways, keeping a low profile and hoping to maintain my relative invisibility. Why? So that Madison and her posse of mean girls would miss me and leave me alone. They loved nothing better than to publicly humiliate me. Their crowning achievement was grabbing me as I walked into the girl's room and flushing my head in the toilet. They held me down until I could barely hold my breath in the cold water. I could hear them laughing their heads off as I finally managed to push them off me and gasp a breath of air. I was soaked, cold and humiliated. "Hey Fiona, didn't you know that the pool is in 'A' wing? Maybe the cold water will do something for that stringy hair of yours!" The bell rang, and they flounced off in their little cheerleading outfits, giggling like crazy, with pom-poms in tow. I squished off to the principal's office to report the incident.

Mrs. Adelson was the bitchy middle-aged woman who served as the principal's secretary. She had badly permed brown hair, glasses on a gaudy chain around her neck, and no waist. She was totally cylindrical from her neck to her knees. The dangerous combination of wet shoes and a highly waxed office floor literally threw me off balance. With flailing arms I skidded into the office and flopped unceremoniously onto the high counter. Mrs. Adelson glared at me, as that counter was the safety barrier between her and the unsavory teen population that she dealt with daily. Clearly, I was invading her space. "What happened to you and what do you want?"

"Madison Chambers and her band of evil dwarfs ambushed me in the second-floor girl's room and flushed my head in the toilet."

"Madison is a model student and would *never* do such a thing! Stop fooling around, Fiona. You're due in the auditorium right now to run through your valedictory address. You're supposed to be representing the class of 1980—God help us. GO!"

Feigning dignity, I smoothed back my soggy tresses, slouched and squished down the hall to the auditorium.

So here I stand, all these years later, a grown woman who, when faced with a specter from the past, is reduced to that pitiful teenaged girl. The ironic thing is that, if asked to recount that episode which still makes me wince in pain, Madison would doubtless not even remember it.

I tell myself that I should hold my head proudly and march up to her door to collect the bags of clothes that she is donating to our church rummage sale. By all accounts, I am accomplished. I breezed through college at Princeton and grad school at Harvard and had a Ph.D. in Psychology by the time I was twenty-five. I worked as an analyst for the FBI and was often involved in joint projects with Homeland Security and sometimes the CIA. I was somewhat of an expert on domestic terrorism and was their top profiler. I was asked to spend some time in Israel, to learn profiling, security techniques and protocols. I particularly enjoyed my time there, and as part of my research, went through El Al's sky marshal training program. I emerged from that with a permanently heightened eye for detail and deduction. The Israeli's are masters of profiling and counter terrorism.

My career went into stasis when, after more than a year of eighteen-hour days following the 9/11 attacks, I needed to distance myself from the horrors that I'd been analyzing. I decided to become a stay-at-home mom for my rapidly growing son, and a volunteer in the community that I had never gotten a chance to know. Hence the trip to Madison's house for her clothing donation to my church's rummage sale. She had told me to ring the front door bell and if there was no answer, to go around back into her kitchen. The door would be unlocked, and the clothes would be in bags at the foot of her rear staircase. So, who the hell locks their front door and leaves the back door unlocked? Seriously? Oakwood is a nice New Jersey suburb, but we're not in Kansas!

My bright red Converse high tops plodded up the tidy front steps, and I smoothed the front of my *I'm a Rutgers University Mom* hoodie before ringing the bell. I couldn't help but think that perhaps I should work a bit on my personal style. Maybe I could buy some of Madison's donations. She would no doubt be casting off some used Prada and Gucci clothes and if I was really lucky, maybe a couple of pairs of Christian Louboutin pumps. Hey, I'm not proud. I wouldn't mind looking stylish for a reasonable price and with a son in college, this is my only hope for high style. I reminded myself to look in the bags when I dropped them off at church.

Hmmm, no answer at the front door, so around the back I went. I knocked but there was no answer. I opened the door slightly and yelled, "Hey Madison, are you home?" No answer, so I stepped in and started heading for the bags at the bottom of her stairs. From the corner of my eye, I saw a figure at the table in the breakfast nook. It was Madison, slumped over. Her chest was lying in her blueberry pancakes—wow that stain will never

come out of her cream Chanel jacket! Her nose had landed
directly in her coffee cup. I knew that she was dead—I'd seen
dead bodies many times before. I tried to find a pulse in her limp
wrist, but as I suspected, there was none. I thought to myself,
*Hell, she looks better dead than I do alive! I'm still embarrassed
in her presence—I need to go back to therapy!* I pulled out my cell
phone and dialed 911.

CHAPTER 2

"**9**11, WHAT'S YOUR emergency?"

"I'm at 211 Elmwood Avenue and upon entering the home, I discovered the homeowner to be unresponsive. I'm requesting police and the coroner. Come around to the back door by the kitchen."

"What do you mean by unresponsive?"

"I mean dead."

"I'll send the ambulance and police. Only medical professionals are qualified to determine a death. Are you a doctor?"

"I am."

"What is your specialty?"

"Psychology."

"So, you're a shrink and you want to pronounce a woman dead? The ambulance is on the way. Stay with the patient and be encouraging and positive when speaking to her and I'll remain on the line."

I turned to Madison and said, "You just stay right there and relax, help is on the way." There, was that positive enough? I set the phone down and decided to have a quick look around the house since I had a few minutes. I had a pair of surgical gloves in the pouch of my hoodie since I was collecting a lot of donations that day and frankly sometimes the stuff is just dirty.

I walked around the kitchen where you could literally eat

off the floor. The house was so clean that it looked like a model home—just for show but not lived in. I opened the fridge. Only healthy foods lined the shelves. Nothing had an expired sell-by date. Really? Everyone has expired food in their fridge . . . don't they? I moved on to the living room, dining room and laundry room. At a quick glance, nothing stood out as unusual. I only had another minute or two, so I ran up the stairs and headed to the master bedroom. From experience I knew that I could glean the most information about a person from their bedroom, bathroom, office and kitchen.

I went directly to the master bathroom and looked through the medicine chest. There were no prescriptions in there. None. Just the usual toothpaste, floss, comb and skin care. Seriously? She has the whole line of La Mer? I couldn't even afford the bottle caps in that line. I looked through the drawers in the vanity. There was a blow dryer, flat iron, hair care products, body lotion and shower gel. Nothing special. I closed the drawer as I heard the sirens coming down the street. I sprinted down the hall and down the stairs. Popping off the gloves, I stood casually in the kitchen just as I saw the EMTs and police heading to the house.

The first to come through the open back door was a short, round, middle-aged police officer who introduced himself as Officer Sorinni. The paramedics followed him over to the body.

"Are you the one who made the 911 call?" he asked as he approached me with opened notebook in hand.

"Yes. I'm Dr. Fiona Wakefield. I came over to pick up some rummage sale donations for Prospect Church. I found Madison, uh, Ms. Chambers just as you see her, when I came in to pick up those bags." I pointed to the two black plastic trash bags sitting at the foot of the stairs to the upper floor.

"I have a number of questions for you, Dr. Wakefield." Just as he was about to continue, the paramedic who was standing over Madison said, with an element of surprise and annoyance, "She's dead sir."

"Don't move the body. Go ahead and call the coroner and I'll give Detective Green a call."

He glanced at me and said, "You're a doctor and you didn't know that she was dead?

"I DID know." I said in my own defense.

"Then why didn't you say so in your 911 call? You're wasting valuable emergency time."

"Play the 911 tape and you'll hear that I said that she was unresponsive—dead. The 911 operator chose not to take my word for it."

He looked at me the same way that you look at the bottom of your shoes when you've just squished into something that your dog left on the lawn. He then pulled out his cell phone. "It's time to bring in the crime scene guys. I'm calling Detective Green." He dialed, "Stew, hey, this is Nick Sorinni. How ya doin'? Yeah, fine, can't complain . . . and if I did who'd listen, right?" He broke into snorts of laughter. Clearly a man who can crack himself up, I thought. How special.

"Yeah, so Stew, I have a deceased middle-aged Caucasian female at 211 Elmwood Avenue. How long before you can come over and take a look around? Ten minutes? Perfect. See you in a few." He clicked off the phone and returned his attention to me. Meantime, the paramedics wandered back outside to wait for the coroner's van to arrive.

"Dr. Wakefield, what type of medicine do you practice?" Officer Sorinni asked as he readied his pen to take notes.

Here we go again, I thought. "I have a Ph.D. in Psychology. I was a profiler and agent with the FBI for many years, so this isn't the first dead body that I've identified even though I'm not a medical doctor." I waited for a look of disgust to cross his face. Boom—I got it.

"So I see why the 911 operator blew you off. Really, YOU have a PhD and worked for the FBI? You realize that we'll have to verify that." He looked at me as though I was not only telling a big one, but would also roll him for his lunch money in a heartbeat. He continued, "So do you want to tell me why you just wandered into a lady's house to pick up clothes?"

"I grew up with Madison Chambers, so I've known her for many years. She knew that my church runs a rummage sale every year in the fall. Every year, around this time, she gives me a call to come by and pick up a donation. She told me to knock on the front door, and if there was no answer, to go around to the back. She said that the door would be open and to just walk in and take the two black trash bags that were at the bottom of her stairs. As I did that, I saw Madison, realized that she was dead, and called 911."

"So, she was a friend?"

"Friend would be stretching it a bit. She was a schoolmate and a fellow member of the community. We didn't socialize, if that's what you were wondering."

"Sounds like you didn't like her much. Did you have anything against her?"

"Do you mean did I have a reason to kill her? No. She was not very nice to me while we were in school, but that was years ago, and we were kids. I was only here to pick up a church donation."

"When did you get here? Did anyone know that you were coming here? Did anyone see you enter the home?"

"I got here at exactly 9:15, because the DJ on the radio station that I was listening to in the car announced the time and gave a traffic report. I looked at my watch to make sure that it was exact, and it was. My son knew that I was coming here, as did the rummage sale workers. They are standing by at the church like a flock of vultures, ready to pick through Madison's donation bags. She has great stuff and it's an annual event to sort out her rummage! The neighbor next door saw me come in. She was watering her lawn and we said good morning to each other as I walked to the back door."

"You know that I'll have to verify all of this information," he said flatly.

"Yes, I know. You might find it helpful to check the feeds from Madison's surveillance cameras. She has one at each corner of the property's perimeter and one at each door. My guess is that with that number of personal surveillance cameras, the deceased has quite a computer set up to monitor them. There's also a camera at the ATM at the bank across the street, and a traffic cam at the intersection."

"How did you even know all that?" Sorinni said with a stunned look.

"It's what I do." Thankfully, before he could grill me further, the coroner's van pulled up and the coroner, with traditional doctor's bag in tow, walked through the back door.

"Atlee," I exclaimed as I walked over to her, arms stretched wide.

"Doc," she squealed back. We hugged like old friends who hadn't seen each other in way too long . . . which we were!

"You guys know each other?" said the dazed Officer Sorinni.

"We're sisters from other mothers," laughed Atlee. Officer Sorinni was now confused and pale. A five-foot tall black coroner had just told him that her sister was a five-foot-six white woman!

"Officer Sorinni, Doc is my oldest and dearest friend. We grew up together and were inseparable. We spent so much time at each other's houses that our parents barely knew what girl belonged to which family. The parents joked that we were sisters. We went to college together and even went to the same grad school. Think of it as nerd bonding."

Looking at me, the officer managed, "So you look less and less like someone who is involved here."

Atlee jumped in, "Involved in what? I haven't even looked at the body. We need to determine if the death is from natural causes or suspicious circumstances." She walked over to the body, placed her bag on the floor and put on her surgical gloves. She moved Madison's head sideways to look at her face. Madison's eyes were wide open, staring straight ahead. Yet she looked peaceful and not at all panicked. Atlee examined Madison's neck and continued to look around the body. She picked up her wrist, then replaced it.

With help from one of her assistants, Atlee lifted Madison from the chair and laid her on a body bag that had been arranged on the kitchen floor. She then inserted a probe into Madison's liver, which determined its temperature. From that she would have a rough estimate of the time of death. She walked outside to have a word with the paramedics, then sent them on their way, and called over her assistant to bring in the gurney and give her a hand. She walked back into the kitchen and addressed Officer Sorinni, "This woman appears to be in top physical form. There seems to be no sign of a struggle. I estimate that she's been dead for about eight to ten hours. I'll be able to confirm that and tell you much more once I can get her to the morgue and examine her." She turned to me. "Something doesn't seem to track here. My gut tells me that this is a suspicious death." Then looking out the window she added, "Oh hey, the posse has arrived, here comes Green."

A very plain, tall man with gray hair, gray suit, gray shirt and a gray tie walked in. Thank God he had a detective's badge on his jacket pocket, as it was the only thing that brightened him up. Otherwise he'd look like the fog rolling in.

"Hey Stew," said Atlee with a smile.

"Hey Atlee. Officer Sorinni," he said nodding to them both. "What do we have here?"

"I'll brief you, Sir," said the officer

"Fine." Looking at me he said, "And you are?"

Before I could answer, Atlee said," This is my friend Dr. Fiona 'Doc' Wakefield who found the body. She's made a statement and will be available for further questioning. In the meantime, she'll be with me and will be assisting on the case."

"She will?" said Detective Green

"She will?" said Officer Sorinni

"I will?" I said.

"Absolutely!" said Atlee with her customary determination. Then to me she said, "Walk with me, I need to talk to you." She picked up her bag and we walked outside. She turned to me and said, "Life has gotten busy for both of us and we haven't seen each other in way too long."

"I know. I'm so sorry that I've let the months slip by."

"When did your house burn down?"

"What? No, no. My house is just fine!"

"So those clothes weren't given to you because you had nothing to wear? Girl, you chose those clothes? Have mercy!" She tugged at my baggy sweatshirt and looked at my mom jeans and Chuck Taylor high tops. She froze when she saw the collar of a plaid flannel shirt peeking out from under the neck of the hoodie. Then she added, "You know that I don't wear plaid flannel. And here's a tip, you shouldn't either. Thank God your mom and my mom didn't live to see you dressed like that, cause it would have killed them!"

"Since I stopped working, I may have lost my way a bit fashion-wise."

"Lost your way? Sweetie, you are adrift in a fashion wasteland. You were an actual fashionista when we were in college. Even when you worked for the FBI you had it together with those dark pants suits and white shirts. It was dull and up tight, but still sort of government chic. Honey, what size are you under all of that?"

"I don't know. I've lost some weight but haven't been out to buy new clothes in a long time."

"You're telling me! Here's the thing. If you're going to be working with me, you're going to have to look professional. It's ten thirty now. Go to the mall and buy a couple of work outfits. The fashion will come back to you, don't worry. It's like riding a bike." She reached into her purse and pulled out a business card. "Call this number and get in to see my hairdresser today. Tell her that I sent you. Get that 'naturally blond' hair with the mile-long roots touched up. Be in my office at nine a.m. tomorrow and we'll get to work.

"About that –"

"There is no 'about that.' You've been letting your brain and your entire *self* hibernate for way too long. You need to work, and I need your help. Something hinkey is up with Madison and I know that you're the one to find out what. I also know that you had plenty of time to look around that house while you were waiting for emergency services to arrive. What did you notice? I know that you did that 'thing' you do – you know, looking around and taking mental Polaroids. You have a mind like a steel trap."

Noting Green and Sorinni staring at us through the kitchen window, I told Atlee that I'd fill her in on what I'd noticed at our meeting the next day.

CHAPTER 3

I T SEEMED UNUSUAL to be back in the old routine of being shocked out of bed by the Bose Wave System blaring rock music at 7 am. I've always hated the incessant beep of alarms, so I go with classic rock. This morning, I danced downstairs to the Stones pounding out "Gimme Shelter." Ah, what a way to start the day!

After a high fiber breakfast, handful of assorted vitamins and minerals and an IV of coffee, I danced back upstairs to get ready for my first day of work in several years. I did exactly as Atlee had *strongly* suggested—okay, ordered. I'd gotten my "natural" blonde hair touched up and trimmed, and had gone to the mall for a couple of classic wardrobe basics. I popped off the Hello Kitty sleep shirt that my son had given me for Christmas when he was five, and began to dress. I chose a Ralph Lauren black and white striped shirt, black pencil skirt, and black pumps. I tied an equestrian printed silk scarf around my neck in an ascot style. Hair combed, contacts in, and subtle makeup on—let's step back and take a look. Holy shit! It turns out that I really do clean up pretty well. My jaw dropped as I stared at myself in the full-length mirror. Under those mom jeans, hoodies, and Chuck Taylor high-tops lurked a size two woman who looked as if she could have been staring out from the pages of the Ralph Lauren Catalogue. Good. I'm road ready.

The traffic moved along at a slow pace on this sunny Monday morning. I pulled into the hospital parking lot, parked, and entered the main lobby. The décor was not that of a sterile old hospital of the past but rather an upscale trendy hotel. Over-stuffed armchairs and glass-topped coffee tables were arranged in cozy sitting areas. A complimentary Keurig coffee and tea station was set up on a console table steps away from the concierge desk. Floor to ceiling windows on two walls brought in cheery sunlight and a view of a treed hillside that was rare for this side of the city.

I walked over to the information desk where a fresh-faced smiling young woman greeted me. "Hello, my name is Meghan, how may I direct you?"

"I wonder if you could tell me where to find the coroner's office, Dr. Atlee Carney."

"Coroner?" Meghan asked quizzically.

"She's in charge of the morgue, so I'm betting that her office is probably in the basement," I said, hoping that this clue would flip on the light switch behind Meghan's now dim eyes.

"What's the morgue?" she asked.

Now there was a neon sign flashing "moron alert" in my brain but I bit my tongue, took a breath and regrouped. I looked at her nametag, which read Meghan Woods, Communications and Customer Service Intern. Intern, God let's hope that it's an unpaid internship.

I pressed on. "So, Meghan, I see that you're an intern. Let me guess, you'll be off to college in a few weeks and I'll bet that you're going to be majoring in communications."

"OMG! How did you even know that?" she asked in disbelief.

"Well, the backpack on the floor behind you says *Way To Go Columbia H.S. Class of 2017*, so I assumed that you've just graduated. Your nametag says communications intern, so I figured you found an internship that would give you experience in an area of interest that just might be your future college major. Let me take it a step further. I'll also bet that your mom arranged for you to have this internship, as I noted a Marie Woods on the plaque listing hospital trustees. You look just like Marie. How did I do?"

"You're exactly right on all counts! You must be psychic or something."

"No, just observant. So, may I ask where you'll be going to college?"

"Harvard!" she chirped. "Just between you and me and the trees, my SAT's weren't exactly what they were looking for, but my dad chatted with them and they decided to accept me anyway. Dad went there too, so he must have known who to talk to."

"I'm quite sure he did. Your dad wouldn't be Senator Woods, would he?"

"Yup, sure is. Wow ma'am, you really ARE psychic!"

My heart sank. My alma mater. Oh Harvard, what hast thou done? Oh well. In a few years, there would be a Woods Endowed Chair of Communications or a Woods Gallery or a Woods Academic Center on campus, so all was not lost.

"Good luck, Meghan!" And to myself, "Good luck Harvard!"

Then I added, "I'll go down to the basement where I'm sure that I'll find Dr. Carney's office. By the way, the morgue is where they store dead people."

"EWWWWWWW!" squealed the horrified Ivy Leaguer.

I stepped onto the elevator. My work there was done.

CHAPTER 4

THE ELEVATOR DOORS opened, and I stepped into a white-tiled hallway filled with bright light and the strong smell of disinfectant. A sign on the wall in front of me indicated that the morgue and coroner's office were toward the left. I clicked down the hallway in those stupid heels that I was sure were necessary since I had meetings on my first day of work and needed to look "professional." So now the new and improved "professional" me stood outside the heavy stainless steel and glass automatic doors of the morgue. A red emergency light and alarm were above the door and security cameras were mounted strategically at hallway corners and on the ceiling outside of the morgue entrance. So much security for dead people—could we call it "over kill?" Oh crap, there I was, making those stupid mental jokes I make when I'm nervous.

As I approached, the doors slid open. I scanned the room and was reminded that decorating exclusively with stainless steel is a very clean yet minimalistic look. Four autopsy tables were lined up next to each other in front of me and on the wall facing me were ten refrigerated drawers. On the wall to the left of the doors behind me were x-ray viewers and a Spartan desk and chair. The wall to the right of the doors was full of storage cabinets with counter tops and sinks below. In both back corners of the room flanking the drawers were offices. The one on the right said Forensics—Dr. Louisa Maria Christina Vollari. That name rang a bell. It was the name of a powerful crime family in the area, headed by Vinny Vollari, or V Squared, as he was known. Nah—that's just crazy. My inner field agent was getting the better of me. No one connected with them could possibly be the star of a crime lab.

Shaking that thought, I turned to a collection of old forty-five records that framed the doorway to the office on the left. First was "Two Tickets to Paradise" by Eddie Money, then "Last Dance" by Donna Summer followed by "Highway to Hell" by AC/DC and finally my favorite, "Stairway to Heaven" by Led Zeppelin. Through the half-opened door, I spotted two signs mounted on the back wall. One was a highway sign that read "Last Exit" and the other an old motel sign that noted "Check Out Here." I'd forgotten about morgue humor—dark, but you have to admit, funny.

I walked over to the office door labeled Coroner—Dr. Atlee Carney. Muted strains of Jimmy Buffett singing "Margaritaville" floated out to greet me. I knocked on the door and Atlee's familiar voice called out "If you're out there wearing your stupid red high tops, you can just leave them outside the door."

"Nope, I'm wearing my stupid black heels that are killing my feet," I grumbled.

"Ok, then you are granted entrance—come on in."

I opened the door and just about dropped my teeth. There was Atlee, sitting behind a rattan glass-topped desk, the desk chair upholstered in a vivid orange Hawaiian print. Behind her was a wall of floor-to-ceiling bookcases rimmed in tiny Christmas lights. The rattan couch on the left wall had the same Hawaiian upholstery and assorted throw pillows that said "Surfin' USA," "California Dreamin'," and "Beach Blanket Bingo." In front of the couch was a glass-topped wicker coffee table covered with framed photos of family and friends. The walls were covered with the requisite diplomas, certifications, awards and professional memberships. Above the door to a connecting office was an enormous stuffed and mounted sailfish. The plaque said "Ramon, July 15, 2002." There was a hanging skeleton with several fake floral leis around his neck and a coat tree with two starched lab coats, two sets of acid green scrubs, and two pairs of orange Crocs in the corner behind the door. The whole room smelled like a tropical drink,

"Dried banana chip or mango?" Atlee said as she offered the Tupperware container of dried fruit.

I took a banana chip and absently crunched away as I tried to find words. "So, what the hell is this? It looks like a set for a Don Ho show in Vegas."

"Ah ha. You're the profiler, so just to get you back in practice, you tell ME what the hell this is."

I took a deep breath and began. "OK. Well, the books and diplomas are the grounding forces here—they are tools of the trade. You surrounded the books in lights for two reasons. One they are enlightening, and two you just like the funky twinkling colors. The tropical theme—Hawaiian prints, quirky fun pillows, rattan and wicker—all remind you of your favorite places on earth and the best times that you've had with family and friends. The pictures on your coffee table bear that out. All are full of smiling faces, beautiful places—clearly depicting everyone you care for—all showing affection for one another, the pure joy of being together and loving life. The skeleton with the leis shows that you've given a light touch to another reminder of your job. Even your choice of scrubs and Crocs are hot, uplifting colors. So why is the fish named Ramon?"

Atlee smiled, "The family took a trip to the Gulf Coast and we spent a day deep sea fishing in the Gulf of Mexico. I caught Ramon and after quite a struggle, reeled him in. I don't know—I thought he deserved a truly Mexican name."

"I must say that taxidermy is a particularly effective decorating medium."

"Wise ass!"

"Anyway, my quick assessment is that your office is your "happy place." You have an intense job and you work hard to give victims the justice they deserve by finding out what happened to them in their last minutes. You are surrounded by death, often quite violent death, every day, so you need a space that grounds you in life. You need balance. In my opinion, you've done exactly the right thing."

"Well, you nailed it. Now it's my turn to ask you a few questions before we get started today. Tell me what happened to you after 9/11. I need to know, as a friend and as a colleague."

"I worked eighteen-hour days for over a year, investigating, analyzing and reporting on the terror attacks. I can't tell you all the details because most of what I did is still classified. I can say that I was sent to examine the three attack sites—I mean up close and personal—full Hazmat gear. The things I saw I wouldn't wish on anyone. I interviewed survivors, first responders, airport personnel and victim's families. I researched terror networks and followed money trails. Finally, I compiled a fifteen hundred-page report and debriefed everyone from Homeland Security and Pentagon officials to the White House and Congress. When the pieces came together and the whole picture of terrorism and the future of our national security came into focus, I was mortified—it was chilling. I've profiled these terror groups and let me assure you that for them there are no rules, no boundaries and worse, there is no respect for human life. I finally realized that I needed to step away from it all and regroup in my own "happy place." I needed to spend time with my family and I needed to become part of my community again in order to regain perspective. I've done that and now I'm ready to get back to work. Thanks for giving me the push I needed to return."

Atlee smiled. "Thanks for being so candid about your work during the 9/11 investigation. I knew that you'd been through an intense time, but had no idea just how intense it actually was. You have a great mind, and I need your help, not just with this case but also with cases going forward. I've spoken to Police Commissioner Martin about adding you to the team here, but he has a bigger job in mind. He said that he was getting in touch with FBI Director Vale and that they'd be in touch with you today. Meantime, I want you to meet Stitch."

Exactly on cue, there was a knock on the door and a short woman with *big* brunette hair and gold earrings the size of Hula Hoops popped her head into the office. "Hey, you must be Doc! It's so nice to meet you . . . Atlee talks about you all the time. I'm Stitch. Well, officially I'm Dr. Louisa Maria Christina Vollari, but you can imagine that a nickname would come in handy with a name like that." She took a quick breath before she turned blue and continued. "So why am I called Stitch you may ask? Well, in addition to being a forensic scientist, I'm also a forensic pathologist, so I can conduct autopsies. I pitch in when we have a backlog of 'guests' here, assist from time to time and fill in when Atlee goes on vacay. Anyway, I love to 'close' when we're done. You see, my grandmother was a seamstress in Italy, and she did the most beautiful hand stitching. She taught me, so my sutures are really quite nice."

Atlee nodded with evident pride. "Funeral homes always give us compliments on the lovely appearance of our corpses."

"How nice for you," was all that I could manage. Both women beamed. What a very special place this will be to work, I thought as I squeezed out a smile.

Stitch continued, "Now in the interest of full disclosure,

I must mention that my dad is the head of the Vollari crime family. You might wonder about my possible affiliation. Well, Dad and I had a chat when I was about to go off to college. He offered to groom me to head the family business upon graduation, as I was the eldest child and smarter than my two brothers. I declined, telling him that I wanted to be a doctor and go into forensics. Clearly there was going to be what might be considered a 'conflict of interest' when our two worlds collided. Ya know, my working in the morgue on the people that he put there. We made a deal, so to speak. I would work here in the Tri-State Area. He would keep his legitimate business ventures here and transition his more creative ventures down to Florida and the islands where frankly he launders his money. I've been working here for twenty years with no conflict—Dad is a man of his word."

"Alrighty then," I said, nearly dizzy from the vast information dump that Stitch had buried me under in less than five minutes. I saw her take a breath, which meant that she was reloading for another filibuster. Just then, my cell phone rang and the caller ID simply said FBI. I knew that it was Director Vale's office calling. "Excuse me, I just need to take this call," I said as I slipped outside the office.

In the hallway, I clicked on the call. "This is Liz Waites calling from Director Vale's office. The Director would like to meet with you today. He said to tell you that it would be the usual meeting place arranged in the usual way. We are aware of your current location. The meeting is scheduled for ten o'clock. Does that work with your schedule?"

"Yes, that's fine."

"All right then. The Director is looking forward to speaking with you. Have a nice day, goodbye."

"Goodbye," I said and clicked off the phone.

I popped back into Atlee's office. "So, the FBI already has

me on their radar and I have a meeting with the Director in ten minutes. They certainly aren't letting any moss grow under these pumps," I said with a laugh.

"Hey, they want you back in a big way. I don't know what they have in mind for you, but when I spoke to the Police Commissioner about having you on this case, he was thrilled that you were going to be working with us. He apparently hopped on the phone to his old buddy Director Vale as soon as he finished talking to me." Then, walking over to the coat rack and slipping off her lab coat, she revealed bright purple scrubs. Atlee turned to me and said, "You'd better hit the dusty trail. Meantime back here at the ranch, I'll get the autopsy started on Madison. I've taken all the x-rays and sent the blood work off for a full toxicology screen. Let's see what good old Maddy has to 'say' to us."

"Ok. Catch ya later. Very nice to meet you, Stitch," I said as I started to click clack back down the hall in those stupid shoes. Already, I missed my high tops.

I made my way up to the lobby and out the front door of the hospital. Walking down the hill toward the multi-level car park, I felt that I was being followed. The reflection in the plate glass window to my right revealed a large SUV driving slowly behind me. I glanced at my watch. Ten o'clock on the dot. My meeting had arrived, so to speak. I stopped and looked back over my left shoulder. The tinted SUV window partially slid down and a voice said, "Please get in."

CHAPTER 5

THE HUGE SUV stopped and a tall gentleman in a grey suit got out of the passenger seat and came around to open the back door for me. As he reached for the door handle, his jacket moved to reveal a standard issue Glock 22. He opened the door and I stepped up onto the running board. My pencil skirt and I gracefully slid into the back seat.

"Well Doc, are you ever a sight for sore eyes," exclaimed FBI Director Keith Vale as he leaned in to give me a hug and a kiss on the cheek. I kissed his cheek and smiled warmly at my old friend. "You finally gave in and returned to the fold, huh? I knew that I'd wear you down sooner or later. I never missed an opportunity to 'encourage' you to help us again—notes on Christmas and birthday cards finally paid off?"

"Of course they did!" I said smiling, as my eyes rolled up to the ceiling and I gently shook my head. The car pulled away from the curb and our portable meeting began.

Keith continued. "Let me ask you a few things before I delve into the details of what I have in mind. I know that we've chatted many times, about your reasons for stepping away from the agency after your analysis, profiles, and projections following the 9/11 terror attacks. I probably would have done the same thing had I been in your shoes, so I get that. I want to know how you've been since Steve passed away. After his funeral, you seemed to go into hibernation, or at least fell out of regular contact with many of your friends."

"Well," I began, "It was all such a shock. I went to the grocery store on a beautiful Saturday morning and came home to find him dead on the bathroom floor. No warning. He had a massive coronary—that was it. I've spent the last two years, just re-grouping and standing by my son as he finished high school and started college. Not having his dad around is devastating to Chuck and I wanted to be there for him at this real turning point in his life. He's strong and so am I. We've both been able to put our lives back on track and are slowly moving forward. You've been such a supportive godfather to Chuck. We both thank you so much for that. I'm happy to be getting back to work. It's time that I have a new focus—and a regular paycheck," I chuckled.

"Ok, that's all I wanted to know." Keith reached over and picked up a box that had been sitting on the seat next to him. "Here ya go. These have been selected specifically for you."

I opened the box and saw a Glock 19 Gen 4 handgun and an FBI badge. This one didn't denote Special Agent, as did my old badge. The new badge said FBI Tri-State Task Force and the badge number was 0001. I looked quizzically at Keith. "Thank you. This is my favorite Glock! It packs quite a kick, but fits my hand perfectly, so I can easily handle it. Now would you like to tell me what the badge means?"

"I want you to head the Tri-State Task Force. It's an all new division, a collaborative effort between FBI, police, coroners' offices, forensics and courts in New Jersey, New York and Connecticut. We have all three governors on board and we're federally sanctioned so that we have access to the highest levels of government and can easily enlist the services of Homeland and State if need be. You probably don't know this but your 9/11 report literally shook the halls of government and put you on the map. It made clear the fact that we have a gap in law enforcement and investigation in the Tri-State Area. We have similar gaps in other major metro areas, but this Task Force is our prototype. We've been laying the groundwork for several years. When you agreed to assist with the Chambers' death investigation, we felt that we had the perfect opening to approach you. All cases won't have national implications, but of course some will. The current case is high profile because of Ms. Chambers' social status, but also significant because of her powerful connections nationally and internationally."

"So, who are the key players that you've identified for the team?"

"Your friend Dr. Carney and her assistant Dr. Vollari, Detective Green, Commissioner Martin, District Attorney Andrew McCallister and you. You'll report directly to me and so you'll have my direct line as well as those of the three governors. Remember, this is not the political desk job that these positions usually boil down to. I want to tap into all of your talents, so I want you in the field too—doing what you do best. What do you think?"

"I'm honored to be a part of this. I will absolutely never let you down. Thank you for the confidence that you've placed in me. Holy shit, what's this?"

We had pulled up outside of an uber modern brick facility— so new that the workmen were still hustling about finishing various instillations. Camera surveillance was everywhere. Two armed guards approached the SUV as we pulled up to the barricade and IDs were verified.

"This is your new office. Like it?" said Keith as the heavy metal garage door opened and we drove into the underground parking garage.

CHAPTER 6

ATLEE AND STITCH were still working on the autopsy when I returned to the morgue after my tour of the new Task Force facility now nicknamed "The Hub." They were working so diligently they didn't even know that I had entered the room and was standing on the opposite side of the long stainless-steel autopsy table. "Hey," I said, and they both jumped a foot.

"You do know that we handle sharp objects like scalpels and saws, right? Surprising the hell out of us isn't a good plan—just sayin'." Atlee said this as she waved the scalpel in her gloved hand. It's cold metal glinted in the bright light above the table.

"Sorry," I said sheepishly. "What have you got?"

"Madison here is the closest thing to Malibu Barbie that you'll ever see."

"Un-freakin' believable," Stitch chimed in.

"First of all, she's in perfect health. No disease, organs are in great shape for her age and unlike most of America, she clearly exercises and eats a healthy diet. She is the perfect weight for her height. That said, she has had the help of every possible technological advancement to enhance her appearance. Let's take the Madison tour, shall we?"

Atlee adjusted the light, and like a professor starting a lecture, began. "Her hair is highlighted and there are very expensive extensions expertly applied."

"Nice job—I know hair," added Stitch.

"Right, now her face. Honey, this girl has been Botoxed and Restylaned within inches of her life—so she's as smooth and wrinkle free as an ice arena. She's also had eyelifts done on both eyes, a nose job and cheek implants. All top of the line work. Now her teeth are the work of a master. She's got a mouth full of veneers—upwards of $35,000 worth of work there."

"Freakin' beautiful! I know my teeth," said Stitch with great admiration.

"Ok, look here. Her neck skin has been tucked up—a little nip and tuck to sculpt her jaw line. Moving down, yes you guessed it—breast implants that, according to her medical records, bumped her up about two cup sizes. Again, top of the line. Now look at these tiny little marks here and here." Atlee pointed to Madison's stomach and hip. "Liposuction. And last but not least, she's had a butt lift and implants to give her a little extra junk in her trunk. Want to see?"

"No thanks, I'll pass on that one," I said flatly.

Atlee continued. "I hope that Maddy here isn't going to be cremated—because honestly with all of the plastic and chemicals in her she would just melt."

"Jeez Atlee, thanks for that visual." I made notes in my ever-present notebook. This information would be a huge part of Madison's profile—and yes, I took my usual mental "photos" of the autopsy. Then I added, "Any visible signs of foul play?"

"Nope. And the x-rays were clean. She never even had a broken bone as a kid. By the way, there were no signs of any other surgeries, no evidence of ever having been pregnant and no signs of any recent sexual activity."

By this time, Stitch had worked her suture magic, and

Madison was beautifully put back together. "Lovely job, Stitch," Atlee said.

"Thanks, now we're ready."

"For what?" I just couldn't imagine what came next.

"Bow your head and cross yourself," said Stitch.

"Huh? I'm not Catholic."

"Doesn't matter. It's our ritual—to show respect for the dead and to let God know that we're on the case. These poor souls no longer have a voice, so it's up to us to give them one. The last person that most of these folks saw was their murderer. The least that we can do is to pray that we can find out who that was and get justice for them."

I could hardly argue with that, so all three of us bowed our heads and crossed ourselves. Madison was wheeled over and slid into her refrigerated drawer. Atlee and Stitch set about cleaning up. I sat down at the small desk to make a few more notes. A few minutes later, the girls walked over to the desk and delivered a little potted orchid plant with a small smiley face balloon stuck in it.

"This is for our new boss," they said in unison.

I stood up and hugged them both. "Thank you, guys! You, and even the FBI have given me such a warm welcome. I truly appreciate it. I really feel like part of the team. Speaking of team, I think I'd better give Detective Green a call and find out where he is with the crime scene." Nothing like hitting the ground running!

CHAPTER 7

THOUGH DETECTIVE STEW Green had the personality of a bowl of oatmeal, a fact to which both of his ex-wives could attest, he was exceedingly good at his job. He had worked his way up through the ranks and had become a highly respected member of the force during the past thirty years. He knew the criminals—and even the marginally bad guys— in the Tri-State Area like the back of his hand. His colleagues admired his tenacity, fairness and ability to get to the bottom of a crime. However, Green was not what you'd call a "people person," so it did take a bit of finesse to work with him.

I'd only met him briefly the other day at Madison's house. I knew that he was on board with the Task Force, so now as his new boss, I needed to contact him and arrange a little face time. I had to get up to speed on the crime scene and we had to begin our "bonding" process. God help me. I dialed his number. "Green? This is Doc Wakefield."

"Oh yeah, the lady in the red Chuck Taylor high-tops who was at the deceased's house picking up garbage."

"That was rummage not garbage."

"Same difference. So, I hear that you're my boss now. That's a slice of happy pie."

"Look Green, where are you now?"

"I'm at the crime scene, if that's what it really is. We're going over some things a second time and still haven't found anything hinkey. The crime scene guys are about to pack up but I'm going to stay and look around a bit more."

"Ok. I'm coming over. I should get there in about five minutes. I want a full debrief and I need to look around too."

"See ya in a few." Green clicked off his cell."

Five minutes later, I parked my car in front of Madison's house and walked around to the back door. I ducked under the crime scene tape and walked over to Green who was standing in the living room. He looked at me as if he'd just seen a ghost.

"You're the red high-top lady? You look better—ya know—good—ya know—fine." He blushed.

We began a cursory check of the downstairs rooms and were in the den when, through the open door, we saw a woman walking into the kitchen. We both drew our weapons. "Police. Put your hands up and turn around slowly," Green ordered.

The seventy-something woman jumped a foot and blurted out, "Oh my God! What the hell is this? You scared me into the next life. Are those guns loaded? For God's sake, put those things down before someone gets hurt."

We lowered our weapons and showed her our badges. Green growled, "It's illegal for you to be in here. Now tell us who you are and what you're doing in an active crime scene. You had to duck the yellow tape to get in—clearly you could see that this area was off limits to the public." I was annoyed but recognized her as the lawn-watering neighbor from next door.

"I'm Eda Stein from next door and I'm here to get what's mine."

"And what would that be, Mrs. Stein?" asked Green.

"The Delft moo-cow pitcher."

"I'm sorry, what?" I said.

"See up there on the second shelf over the glassware?" she

said as she pointed to the cupboard with the glass doors. "That's it."

On the shelf stood a small blue and white pitcher in the shape of a cow. There was a hole in its back where you filled it, the tail was the handle and the snout was the spout so the milk spit out of its mouth. A charming piece.

"I was about to get it for fifty cents at the local flea market, when Madison swooped in and offered a dollar for it. I was willing to go as high as a dollar fifty, but before I could bid, you see, I was checking to make sure I had that much change with me, the dealer sold it to Madison. It was a dark day and I've never gotten over it. I figured that she wasn't going to need the pitcher where she was going—it's hot down there and I'm sure milk would curdle—so I'd just take it."

Green looked dumbfounded, then managed, "Mrs. Stein, you can't just rip stuff off from a crime scene, no matter what the circumstances. I'll make a note that you'd like the pitcher, and those in charge of the deceased's estate can contact you when they dispose of the contents of the house. Meantime, paws off everything here. And no more trespassing—got it?"

The poor woman looked sad and lonely. This was probably the most excitement that she'd had in decades. Finally, she looked at us and said, "You like soup? It's five o'clock now. You'll come over and have soup and rolls. It's chicken noodle and I made it fresh this morning. Come on. You both look skinny."

Shocked, I was about to say no when Green piped up with, "That's really nice. We'd love to join you and maybe chat about the neighborhood and what's been going on here lately."

Mrs. Stein walked ahead through her back door and I grabbed Green by the arm. "What the hell are you doing? We were walking a crime scene, and now we're having supper with a senior citizen with a thing for moo-cow pitchers! Are you crazy?"

"I love homemade soup. My grandmother made it all the time. Besides, Mrs. Stein is harmless and lonely and could use some company. She's also the kind of neighbor who knows everything that goes on here—all we have to do is chat with her and we'll find out a ton. Trust me. Think of this as an interview with benefits. I wonder what's for dessert?"

CHAPTER 8

A S IT TURNED out, Mrs. Stein's soup was great, and she gave us some valuable information—as well as the recipe. On the night of the murder, she woke in the middle of the night, around four a.m., to use the bathroom. Looking out of her bedroom window, which was on the side of the house that faced Madison's, she saw someone dressed in a black hoodie outside the house. They appeared to be looking around the perimeter of the house. Then they walked toward the back and she lost sight of them. Whoever it was, was carrying a small white paper bag—like a fast food bag. She heard nothing more, so she went back to sleep.

Now let's keep in mind, that Mrs. Stein was in her late seventies and didn't have her glasses on. She didn't report anything to the police because she didn't hear a disturbance, and frankly was unsure if what she'd seen was real or part of a dream. She was sharp as a tack and my gut feeling was that she really did see something. The uniforms had canvassed the neighborhood and had come up empty for witnesses or unusual sightings that night. Not much to go on.

Green and I met at Madison's house again the next morning to continue our search. I got there first and decided to look around outside before going in. Why would Madison have so many surveillance cameras around her house? This was a lovely home full of nice things, but hardly a mansion full of Faberge eggs. Maybe she had a lot of expensive jewelry. Every time I saw her, she was wearing pretty much the same things—diamond stud pierced earrings, a string of pearls, a Rolex watch and her mom's emerald ring. She had all of those things on her after the murder. Again, nice stuff but hardly warranting a surveillance system of this magnitude. She also had an advanced alarm system that wrapped the lower rooms of the house in a web of lasers. I'd seen these systems in museums and the very upscale homes of the rich and powerful. Those homes were full of priceless art, jewels to rival the Queen's and insurance policies with Lloyds of London. I never thought Madison was a part of that world, but something wasn't right here. Maybe she was more than she appeared to be.

On the other hand, the upstairs rooms only had lower-grade window alarms, so maybe not. My musings continued as I rustled around in the garden and bushes surrounding her house. She had an unremarkable Trane central air-conditioning system on the side of the house. However, near the rear of the house, almost entirely hidden by bushes was a top of the line HVAC system—one that I had only seen in museums and art galleries. Now I was sure that there was much more to Madison than there seemed!

I heard Detective Green's voice nearby. "Yo, Doc! Where the hell are ya? I know you're out here somewhere. Marco."

"Is this where I'm supposed to say Polo?" I replied to Green, as I made my way out of the bushes and plucked leaves out of my hair. "Really? Marco Polo? You played that game as a kid too?"

"Oh please, all of us of a certain generation did. I'm surprised that you responded though. I figured that you were, you know . . ."

"A prick who pretty much skipped childhood and was actually born an adult?"

"Yeah . . . I mean, no . . . ya know, a deadly serious type 24/7. Anyway, what have you found out here in the wild?"

I told Green about the cameras, HVAC and alarm systems. "Did your guys thoroughly go over this place from attic to basement after they worked the immediate crime scene?"

"They absolutely did and found nothing unusual. I also just heard from the lab guys and they've gone over all the surveillance tapes. Nothing but darkness all night—no movement. Looks like Mrs. Stein was wrong about seeing a middle of the night wanderer out here."

"No, I don't think she was wrong. Let's dig deeper and look for subtle camera blind spots. We're missing a lot here. We need to find more dots to connect. Let's go down to the basement," I said and led the way inside.

We walked through the kitchen to the basement door, flipped on the light and went downstairs. We entered a lovely family-room living area. Indirect lighting all around gave the room a cozy glow. The floors were covered in a latte-colored soft carpet and the furnishings were oatmeal colored over-stuffed couches and chairs. A huge flat screen TV hung on the wall over the gas fireplace. There were handcrafted wooden tables and a modern wet bar with stainless steel sinks, granite countertops and a subway tile back splash. Wine glasses hung on the rack above the sink, and cocktail glasses of all types lined the shelves of the glass-fronted cabinets. A small stainless-steel refrigerator held a few bottles of beer and drink mixes. Through one door there was a beautiful full bath done in the subtle colors of sea glass. Through the other door was a laundry room with shelves for tools and storage.

"Hey, this is pretty sweet! Madison must have done quite a bit of entertaining," said Green.

"That's the thing, she was nearly a recluse. She was seen at charity events, but that was it. She always went to events unescorted. At one point, rumor had it that she was a kept woman, with a rich male friend who bought her designer clothes. That probably started because she had no apparent means of support. She was on the boards of several foundations but that was it. Yet she always dressed as if she had just stepped off the pages of *Town & Country Magazine*. Let's keep looking around here. None of this is adding up for me."

Looking puzzled, Green added, "Designer clothes are pretty pricey, right? Well, we looked at her bank account information and found that she's comfortable, but not rolling in cash. We're in the process of checking investments now, but as for ready cash—not millions. She has no debt—owns the house and owes nothing. Where is she getting her money?"

"I know that she came from a wealthy family, but I think that her folks were divorced, and I know that she was raised by a single mom. She may have something in trust or even foreign accounts. We need to keep digging."

I continued to walk around the room and stopped near the fireplace. I glanced down and noticed that it was not at all connected to a gas line. "This is a fake." I rooted around in the logs and when I moved a small branch at the bottom of the pile, I heard the low hum of a motor and the fireplace popped away from the rest of the wall. It was a hidden door like the ones in the old movies! When opened, it revealed a huge vault door. A digitized keypad and palm reader were on the wall next to it.

CHAPTER 9

The next day

WE HAD TOO many loose ends and needed to gather as a group to put our heads together. Green, Stitch, Atlee and I were the central core of the Task Force. All of our associated teams, technicians, labs, lawyers and bureaucrats revolved around us forming a universe of support.

The FBI Tri-State Task Force, or "3TF" as we were now known, was slowly moving into its sleek new home. In addition to beautiful offices, "The Hub" housed state-of-the-art labs, surveillance equipment, computer this and satellite uplink that. You name it and we had it. I decided on a meeting in the conference room to share what we had so far.

"So, Atlee and Stitch, I know that there was nothing remarkable in the autopsy, other than Madison had a fabulous plastic surgeon. Have you come up with a time and cause of death?"

"We have," Atlee replied. "Madison died of an insulin overdose. Her body had the highest levels I've seen in a long time. She was not a diabetic and for that level of toxicity, she would have to have been injected with it. Stitch and I are literally going over the body with a magnifying glass to find the injection site.

"Check behind her ears—right in the creases where they meet her head," I added.

"Why would you say that?" asked Stitch.

"Years ago, I had a case where that was done. It's worth a shot. Do you have a time of death?"

"Yeah, I do. She died between three and five in the morning."

My mental camera brought up pictures of the crime scene. "Then it's just as I thought—the scene was staged. She was dressed for work. How many people are up and dressed for work in the middle of the night, especially if they don't really work? According to her desk diary, her first appointment that day was a board meeting at the Museum of Modern Art at ten o'clock. And another thing, she was lying in her untouched pancake breakfast. Madison's shelves were full of muesli and oatmeal. She wasn't a big cooked breakfast kind of gal, and knowing her health-nut habits, she wouldn't eat anything that was swimming in maple syrup. There wasn't a dirty pan in sight either. The pancakes looked too perfect — like they were from a fast food place rather than homemade." I was on a roll. "So Green, maybe Mrs. Stein isn't so crazy after all. She thought she saw someone carrying a white fast food bag near Madison's house in the middle of the night. My bet is that same person is our killer."

"Why would the killer stage the crime scene?" asked Stitch.

I began, "They want to create an illusion. It may be to make the time of the crime seem very different from what it actually was. It may be to decoy something else. In the case of some mentally disturbed and dangerous individuals, it may be a whimsical backdrop for a sick game of torture or murder."

Green's mouth dropped open. "Well that's creepy! Jeez! We need to go through Madison's trash and the neighbor's trash. There must be a Styrofoam fast food box somewhere. Maybe we can get some prints. We'll interview all the employees from the local McDonald's. That one's open all night and it's only three blocks away from the house. Doc, you're right—something's up with those surveillance tapes. We'll rank them highest priority and get the high-tech guys to go over them this time."

Green then got everyone up to speed on our other findings at the crime scene. "So, to get access to the vault, we'll need latex replicas of Madison's palms. We'll still need a pass code too. The lab guys dusted the keypad for prints, but it was totally clean. The vault door and security system are both professional grade and tremendously hard to drill or even blow. A pass code would be preferable. Any ideas? We've found no password or code list of any kind in the deceased's belongings or on her computer."

Atlee chimed in, "I have a hunch. I'll check the back of Madison's ring and watch for inscriptions. We might find a meaningful date—never know."

"Good idea," I said.

There was a knock on the door. Parker Grimes, one of our attorneys came in.

"Hi guys. I have a legal update to share. I've been in contact with Madison's personal attorney, Jackson Avery. He is the executor of her estate. He's been the Chambers family's attorney for years, first working with her mom, Frances Ogden Chambers. He seems to remember some changes to her will and is researching that as we speak. Supposedly good old Maddy is worth millions—I mean serious millions—like upwards of sixty million. Avery and I are in the process of tracking down all her assets now. Here's the conundrum. For all her supposed wealth, she lived a modest lifestyle. Her house is worth about six hundred thousand dollars. Local bank accounts total about five hundred thousand and her stock portfolio is worth about a million. Granted, from what I understand, her collection of designer clothes is probably worth more than a million—but we are still far from the amount that she's supposed to be worth. We're currently following some leads with overseas accounts."

"Fine, give me updates. I'm going to finish up some paperwork here, then go back to the crime scene. The advanced HVAC system is there for a reason and so is that incredible surveillance system."

"I'll have those latex replicas of Madison's hands ready in about an hour," Atlee said.

"Thanks, I'm starting to see a picture coming together here but we need a few more pieces."

CHAPTER 10

MEANTIME AT A Mercedes Dealership fifteen miles from the Hub . . .

The pristine two-toned navy and grey 1963 Rolls Royce Phantom V glided to a stop in front of the soaring glass building that housed the Mercedes dealership. The classic old car seemed oddly out of place against this sparkling, modern backdrop. The driver's door opened and a perfectly groomed, middle-aged gentleman in an impeccably tailored grey suit stepped out. He walked back to the rear door and opened it, extending his hand to assist his elderly passenger. "When shall I return for you, Mrs. Worthington?"

Davinia Worthington was a trim seventy-something patrician with shimmering silver hair neatly pulled up in a bun. Her wrinkles decorated a face that was quite lovely and was undoubtedly stunning in its younger days. She wore an expensive brown tweed suit and cream silk blouse with multiple ropes of fine pearls that subtly glinted in the afternoon sun. She accepted the proffered hand with her kid-gloved hand, smiled sweetly and replied, "Oh give me about an hour please, Hamilton." She gracefully slid out of the car and smoothed her skirt. "I'd like to take a short test drive, and if all is satisfactory, I expect that there will be some tiresome paperwork to complete."

"Very well, madam. Shall I help you in?"

"No need for that, thank you very much. I can manage from here. Oh, and you know what to do when you get the call?" He nodded. She placed her circa-1950's brown alligator purse in the crook of her arm and walked a bit stiffly into the dealership as Hamilton maneuvered her car slowly away from the curb.

The cavernous showroom was filled with every possible model of beautiful new Mercedes. Shiny chrome and smooth metallic paint adorned these impressive German exports. Davinia felt the eyes of four salesmen fall upon her and soon they were on their feet and moving towards her like sharks converging upon raw meat. Davinia scanned them all with a look as sharp as a laser.

Immediately, the three weakest fell back, leaving the strongest predator to enter her personal space with hand extended and over-whitened teeth gleaming. "Welcome to Briggs-Rayburn Mercedes. I'm Eaton Briggs. How may I assist you today?" he said in a voice as slick as the motor oil that flowed through his inventory.

"Very nice to meet you, I am Davinia Worthington," she said, thinking what a strain it was going to be to deal with a car salesman. "I should like to purchase a car as a gift for my grandson. I have something quite specific in mind."

"Let me read your mind, madam! A safe and practical SUV for that special young man?"

"No. Actually I'm looking for a McLaren SLR Roadster, in red please."

"I think that I'd better familiarize you with some of the particulars of that car. It is an extremely powerful supercar."

"Zero to sixty in 3.8 seconds, a 5.4-liter super charged V8 engine and a top speed of 208 miles per hour. The fastest car in the world with an automatic transmission." The look of disbelief on Briggs' face was priceless. "This model reminds me of the gull-wing that my late husband and I used to enjoy driving when we were a young couple. I hope that my grandson will enjoy this car every bit as much as his grandfather and I did ours," Davinia said with the faint smile that comes from a fond memory.

"This model is limited and the price tag is $495,000.00. We do have attractive financing. We have one model on the lot. It's silver, but with a few calls, red can certainly be found. Would you like me to take you for a test drive?"

"First of all, young man, I do *not* require financing. I feel that one should only make purchases that one can afford. Therefore, I shall be paying in cash. Further, if you took me for a test drive I would hardly be able to evaluate the quality and handling of the car, so I shall drive. I assure you that a woman of my years is hardly going to push the envelope of the car. I merely want to take a quiet drive."

"Very well, madam. I usually ride along with clients on these drives, but under the circumstances, I think that you can take a quick spin on your own. I'll require a banker to vouch for you. May I have your banker's name and number?'

"Of course. The number is in my phone on speed dial. Shall I put you in touch with Mr. Hamilton?"

"Yes, please."

Davinia scrolled through the list of "favorites" on her smart phone and began her call. "Hello, Mr. Hamilton, Davinia Worthington here. I'm with Mr. Briggs of Briggs-Rayburn Mercedes and he would like to have a word with you. I'm about to take a McLaren for a short test drive. Here is Mr. Briggs."

"Mr. Hamilton, this is Eaton Briggs. Mrs. Worthington is taking the test drive on her own, so you can appreciate that with a car of high value, $495,000.00, I would need a banker to vouch for her just to err on the side of prudence."

"Well Mr. Briggs, I assure you that Mrs. Worthington's liquid assets far exceed $495,000.00. She is a highly valued client of our Personal Banking Division and has been for the more than the thirty years that I've known her. Allowing her to drive the McLaren is not only low risk, it is no risk, I assure you."

"Many thanks, and have a nice day. Goodbye." Briggs hung up the phone and handed it back to Davinia.

"As anticipated, all is in order, Mrs. Worthington. Let me just take a copy of your driver's license, do a cursory credit check, fill out the basic information sheet and we'll have the car brought around for you."

"Thank you so much." Davinia opened her purse and extracted an ancient crocodile wallet from which she took her license and handed it to Briggs. She then took out a silver pen and completed the information sheet as she sat in the VIP lounge and sipped Perrier from a Waterford glass. Briggs copied her license and handed it back, then took the information form and looked it over. He went to his desk, tapped in some information, clicked the mouse a few times and smiled. Picking up the phone, he requested that the roadster be brought to the front parking lot. Rising, he escorted Davinia outside just in time to see it swing around the corner and pull up to the curb. Visibly, it was impressive, but audibly it was fantastic! The deep throaty rumble of its super charged V8 engine spoke volumes about its superb engineering.

"I'll just show you where some of the controls are and how they work. Then when you've adjusted the seat to your comfort, you can enjoy your test drive." Briggs pointed out the lights, radio and dials. He then opened the driver's door and assisted Davinia in.

"Thank you, Mr. Briggs," she said as she adjusted the seat and mirrors. "I shall only take a short spin. If all is satisfactory, which I'm sure it will be, I'll place the order upon my return." Briggs nodded and smiled as Davinia clipped her seatbelt and cautiously pulled out of the parking lot onto the main road.

A mile down the road, she pulled over to the curb and parked. She opened her purse and took out a small electronic scrambler that she magnetically attached to the underside of the car. Then she took out an untraceable burn phone and placed a call. "I'm four minutes out, get ready." She checked the mirrors and gently pulled away from the curb to continue down the road.

The area around the car lot was a weave of major highways, with on ramps, off ramps, access to three major airports, two seaports and the train yards. Passing all these, she continued out of town where the scenery quickly became increasingly rural. A sharp left turn put her on the service road to an airstrip that had been defunct since the Vietnam War era. She pulled onto the cracked, weed-infested tarmac of the runway and watched the speedometer climb as she blasted down at one hundred miles per hour. Slowing, she headed to the far end of the bent chain-link fence where an unmarked eighteen-wheeler was opening its automatic rear doors and sliding out a ramp. She expertly lined up the car and at a spritely clip, flew up the ramp and screeched to a halt as the ramp retracted and the doors closed and locked.

CHAPTER 11

Back at the Hub . . .

I WAS SITTING AT my desk finishing up some paperwork when Nicky Henderson, trusted administrative assistant/ office manager/personal assistant/person who knows everything that goes on in the office, knocked on the door and entered in one smooth movement. "Sorry to interrupt Doc, but you'll never believe what was just reported to us."

Now I'm a calm and simple girl, but whenever someone starts off with "you'll never believe . . ." my Zen begins to dissipate. Take the time when my then-high school-aged son said, "Mom, you'll never believe what Kaitlyn and I did!" Thoughts of my carefully honed "birds and bees" lecture raced through my head. I broke out in a cold sweat as I prayed that I hadn't left out any vital details that might save me from becoming a grandmother right now. In the next split second, I knew that he wouldn't have told me THAT, so without skipping a beat managed a simple "What?"

"We both got into the same college . . . cool right?"

"Right. Very cool." Blood pressure dropping, dropping, dropping . . . normal.

So now what would Nicky drop in my lap? Another terror threat? Bank robbery? Art crime? Assassination attempt?

Madison's murder was top priority due to her high profile, coupled with the fact that there had been no capital crime in this area since the Eisenhower Administration. The citizenry was becoming nervous. However, something major might tip the priority list and bump Madison's case off the top. "What's up, Nicky?"

"Grand theft auto! We're talking a Mercedes McLaren SLR super car valued at $495,000.00. Get this, it was boosted, ah err, *stolen* by a little old lady! The driver's license that she gave them said that she was Davinia Worthington. You guessed it— the license was totally bogus. The owner of the Briggs-Rayburn Mercedes Dealership is just about having a heart attack. The car just seemed to vanish. The traffic cam footage in the immediate area showed the car leaving the dealership and heading about a mile down the expressway. It took Exit 6 and was never seen again. Poof—gone. All traffic cam footage within a three-mile radius of that area was offline."

"And that doesn't seem odd to anyone? Wait. You said offline. Do you know what the lab guys meant by that? Was the footage blacked out or was it frozen?"

"Funny you should put it that way. The lab guys said it was stock still like it was frozen."

"OK. We can put Major Crimes on the case, but tell the lab guys to show me the tapes first thing tomorrow morning. I have a hunch that this is related to the Chambers murder."

"Got it." Nicky's efficiency meter went from zero to sixty and she was off!

I might as well be trying to do paperwork in the middle of Grand Central Station. There was another knock on the door and this time it was Stitch. "I've got those Latex duplicates of Madison's hands for you. They look seriously creepy. Hope they do the trick. Also, Atlee got the inscriptions from Madison's jewelry. The watch was inscribed 'FC to MC' and the ring's inscription was simply 1/30/59."

"Thanks. I'm going over to the crime scene now." I glanced at my watch. "Green should be waiting for me down in the parking garage."

Green and I drove over to Madison's house in near silence. We didn't know each other well enough for banal chitchat or collegial conversation. I think that we both felt a bit awkward, sort of like you do when you're at a cocktail party with a room full of folks that you don't really know—more to the point—folks that you don't really WANT to know. I knew he saw me as an uptight, re-cycled "Fed." I saw him as an unremarkable and basic detective. If I were shopping for a detective in a grocery store, Green would be in the "store brands" aisle sitting on the shelf wrapped in a plain black and white label. Maybe even on sale. So there ya have it. We needed to break the ice. Maybe I could think of some common ground to talk about. Worth a try. "So Green, tell me about your family," I ventured.

"Don't have one. Parents are dead. No siblings. All ex-wives hate me and the feeling is mutual. Sperm were slow swimmers so no kids."

Good God, I thought, way more information than I needed and delivered in less than twenty seconds! Where can I possibly go from here? My personal motto is "to boldly go." Is that quote from Plato? No, it's from Star Trek reruns that I watched on the bar TV at the Lambda Chi Alpha Fraternity house before Friday night parties back in my college days. Not terribly deep but it's my motto nonetheless. So, I boldly went. "My parents are gone too. I'm also an only child. Now I'm a widow. My husband died of a heart attack three years ago. I have a son who is twenty and in college."

"Uh huh." Green replied with as much interest and enthusiasm as you might muster watching snails clean the walls of a fish tank. My attempt at personal warmth complete, my heart leaped at the sight of Madison's house coming into view. It really says a lot when the thought of going over a crime scene seems exciting—even cheery—compared to the company of a colleague. I was starting to see why Green has so many ex-wives. Being married to him must have been magic.

We parked in the driveway and entered the house through the back door. I walked ahead as we crossed the kitchen and went down the basement stairs to the family room. Green's uniformed branch had contacted the alarm company to temporarily disable the alarm system so that we could carry out our investigation without the possibility of setting off lasers and alarms.

The fireplace "door" remained ajar, as we had left it. I swung it fully open to reveal the keypad. I took the silicone replicas of Madison's palms out of a plastic bag and applied the right one to it. Bingo, the next screen appeared and asked for the pin number. On a hunch, I decided to try Madison's mother's ring inscription as the code. The date on the inside of the ring that Madison always wore had apparently been her mom's twenty-first birthday gift and treasured by Maddy. I typed 1-30-59. Bingo once again. The screen flashed, "user verified" and the vault door clicked open. I flicked on the light switch and gasped "HOLY SHIT!

CHAPTER 12

"T HE GARDNER HEIST!" was all that I could get myself to say as my mouth went instantly dry. I was in a total state of shock. "So, this explains the advanced HVAC and security systems!"

"What are you even talking about? What's the Gardner Heist? All I see are a bunch of old, musty paintings . . . honestly, I've seen better at Wal-Mart. I will say that old Maddy has spent a small packet on good lighting. She's also dropped plenty on this digital temperature and humidity monitoring system," he said pointing to a wall-mounted display now wildly fluctuating due to the open door. "But bottom line though, who really cares about this junk?" He closed the door.

"Green, you are a Philistine and a moron!" Oh my God, did I actually say what I was thinking? How many human resource violations did I just commit? I could almost hear the sirens of the Political Correctness Police cars roaring towards me. They'd charge me, and my newly resurrected career would be short lived! What just happened? A thought slid down from my brain like a firefighter down a pole. It bounced off the back of my tongue, careened past my teeth and out into the ozone . . . and boom, there it was, the offensive comment.

Green stopped, straightened himself up, looked me in the eye and said "Philistine, you say? I beg your pardon! Except for

two aunts who lived in Park Slope, my whole family is from
Levittown! And moron? No. No one in my family ever had
more than one wife . . . well not at the same time at least! Jeez,
you Jersey people!"

Alrighty then, Philistine and moron it definitely is! Slightly
stunned and relieved, I continued to walk through this
subterranean art gallery. I peered closely at *The Concert* by
Vermeer. Beautiful. Perfect. Authentic. I had noted every detail
of this work, indeed, of all these works, when I visited the
Isabella Stewart Gardner Museum in Boston years ago. I moved
on to examine the three Rembrandts, *Self-Portrait*, *A Lady and
Gentleman in Black*, and my favorite, *The Storm on the Sea of
Galilee*. All were the real deal. I walked over to the Chinese Ku
(beaker) and Bronze Eagle Finial on display in the corner. Both
real. Next, featured on a massive rear gallery wall were the five
pilfered Degas. Authentic. Finally, there hung Manet's *Chez
Tortoni* and *Landscape with Obelisk* by Govaert Flinck. That
was the entire robbery inventory. There was much more art in
this vast private world, but I would have to examine that later.
For the moment, I was overcome by what I'd seen, and as usual
Green was gawking at me as if I'd lost my last marble.

"So, what the hell, Doc?"

"Green, this old musty stuff, as you call it, is priceless art
worth well over $500 million dollars in today's market. It's all
authentic and was stolen in 1990."

"So, what about this heist?"

"I remember it well. Around one a.m. on the night of St.
Patrick's Day 1990, when all of Boston was wasted, the alarm
in the Gardner Museum's conservation lab went off. When
investigated by the guard, nothing was amiss. A few minutes
later, the alarm went off in the carriage house that was behind
the museum at the time. Again, nothing was amiss. Then the
video cameras showed two men dressed as Boston police

officers at the door. The college student who was on duty at the desk, thought that perhaps the alarms had been set off by an intruder who could still be about. Despite standing orders never to buzz anyone in, he unlocked the door for the "cops." The men asked to speak to all guards on duty, so the student "guard" summoned his colleague to the front desk.

"Upon his arrival, both guards were handcuffed by the fake Boston police officers. Their eyes and mouths were duct-taped. One was handcuffed to a steam pipe in the basement and the other to a workbench there. No one was harmed. The alarms in the museum were all internal, and since the panic button in the guard station was not activated, no real police were summoned during the robbery. The thieves then set about going from room to room, cutting paintings right out of their frames. They removed surveillance tapes and printouts of data from motion detectors before leaving.

"This is history's largest, and to this day, unsolved art theft. The high value speaks to the great rarity of the pieces taken. For instance, Rembrandt's *Storm on the Sea of Galilee* was the only seascape he ever painted. Vermeer's *The Concert* was one of thirty-four existing Vermeers in the world. Consequently, a five-million-dollar reward was announced and remains. The museum's conservators issued a plea to those holding the works, that they protect them from great variations in humidity and temperature (68 degrees Fahrenheit and 50 percent humidity). Sadly, the empty frames of the Vermeer, two Rembrandt's and the Flinck still hang in the Dutch Room of the Gardner Museum. They are a reminder of great loss, yet also of hope that someday they'll be returned. This robbery remains at the top of the FBI's Art Crimes List."

"How do you even know all of that?" Green said, stunned.

"I worked with FBI Art Crimes back in the day. It was a fascinating assignment. I love art and I particularly love the

Gardner Museum. I can't tell you how many happy hours I've spent there, wandering from room to room appreciating that vast collection. It's amazing. But I digress. The art experts who worked with the FBI taught me volumes about verifying art authenticity, art history, provenances and spotting forgeries. They, and our friends at INTERPOL, fully briefed me on major international art dealers . . . and thieves. We universally agree that this was a concierge robbery. A private collector gave those guys a shopping list. Easily more than a billion dollars of art resides in that museum, yet only a few specific pieces were chosen."

My eloquent art lecture completed, I turned to look at Green, expecting his face to register the awe that standing in the presence of such iconic pieces usually elicits. Instead, the Philistine was picking a piece of lettuce out of his teeth. He looked at me and shrugged. "Yeah, whatever. I prefer my art new, not used. This old stuff is musty, and God knows where it's been over the years. Now who do you suggest we call to clear this outta here? If it were up to me, it would be Goodwill!" He snorted with laughter.

"Moving along the same lines of refined living, I suppose you prefer your wine with this year's vintage and a screw top?"

"As a matter of fact, I prefer it in a box. That way I know that it's fresh and easy to open. I don't want to drink some old junk that's years old and costs a ton. Would you pay extra to buy a can of beans that's past its sell by date? Same thing."

I rolled my eyes. Where do I even go with that?

"Ok, back to the situation at hand. You call your local guys and tell them that we have a crime scene within a crime scene and have them guard this place. I'll call FBI Art Crimes and tell them to bring forensics over. They'll need to scientifically verify the originality of the art for the record. We'll eventually have to hire professional art movers to pack this and move it to the HUB while it's considered evidence, before we can release it back to the Gardner."

"Don't you need to call them?"

"I do, but not until forensics is done. It should only take a few hours if we get right on it. Also, let's see if we can activate this uber-fancy alarm system. We need to keep this area absolutely secure. We can't let the press have even the slightest whiff of this or we'll have reporters crawling all over the place."

"Right," said Green as he took out his cell phone and headed upstairs to make a call.

I went upstairs to make my own call to the FBI folks.

"Art Crimes, Agent Black, how can I help?"

"Hey Black, this is Doc Wakefield. How are you?"

"Wow, fine. I haven't spoken to you in a month of Sundays! What's up?"

"Are you sitting down?"

"Yup."

"I found the artwork from the Gardner Heist in a sub-basement of a house that we're already processing as the scene of a homicide."

"*Wait*! You said the Gardner Heist? All of it? I know that you'd know this so . . . is it authentic?"

"Yes, it's all there and it's the real deal. Please send your forensics team over to 211 Elmwood Avenue, Oakwood ASAP. Oh, and keep this very quiet until we can make our verifications and necessary calls."

"I don't freakin' believe it! After more than twenty-five years! Ok, I'm all over it Doc. They should be there in about fifteen minutes. I'll be talkin' to you. Bye."

I stood there for a moment to soak in the gravity of the situation. My profiler training kicked in. I had a strong feeling that Madison was not the art thief mastermind here. The robbery occurred in 1990, which meant that although wealthy, she didn't fit the typical profile of a serious art connoisseur of the level required for this. She was too young. Her knowledge of the national and international art markets and auctions, collections, dealers and industry's "dark underbelly" so to speak, were likely undeveloped. As a matter of fact, Madison was only named to the board of several prominent art museums after her mother had passed away, and she simply carried on for her. Her mom had been a board member and major benefactor for decades. She had been a collector and was considered an authority in upper echelon art circles. Madison never showed much interest. My gut said that it was Mom who did this. Frances Ogden Chambers. Madison didn't have the depth or knowledge to appreciate or want any of this. My guess was that she obviously knew about the robbery, but didn't know how to get rid of the stuff in her basement. Most of us don't know how to get rid of the stuff in our basements, but certainly not if it's priceless stolen art!

I already had my gloves on, so I returned to the sub-basement for a further look around. Green's men were stationed outside, and he joined me downstairs.

"My hunch is that there's another safe down here," I said as I started my search along the walls.

"What for? The whole room is a safe."

"None of the searches have turned up information on bank accounts or personal documents other than the will that Madison's lawyer has. There's either a ton of cash here or the key to a safe deposit box or a number to an international bank account . . . or all of the above."

"I don't know how you just pull this stuff out of the ozone, but fine . . . if you think there's some huge clue here, then we'll root around."

Now that Green had made me feel like a pig digging for truffles, we continued poking around. He peeked behind pictures on the walls while I rolled up the exquisite Oriental rug to look for a floor safe. Neither of us had any luck. The room was vast, with expensive museum lighting, expertly placed to best set off the collection. Sumptuous leather couches and chairs were arranged for relaxing and appreciating the gallery. Beautiful tables with inlaid wood held art magazines, journals, and books. The floors were a parquet of rare woods enhanced by the Oriental rug. It was a rich, serene space.

There was a lovely antique bar in one corner with Baccarat crystal wine glasses twinkling on shelves. Next to that was a door to a temperature-controlled wine room. I entered to find racks upon racks of the finest vintages from around the world. There was at a glance easily ten million dollars' worth of rare and fine wines and cases of champagne. I knew that Madison didn't drink. Her unknown father was said to have been a drunk, albeit a wealthy one, and she had racked up some DUIs during her college days. Her mom put her into rehab and she stayed on the wagon for the rest of her life. So, the wine was an investment. Clearly her mother's carefully curated collection.

I exited the wine room and re-entered the main room. In the far corner there stood a white museum pedestal, which displayed the most breathtaking Ming vase I had ever seen. On a whim, I reached over and picked it up to more closely examine it. As I did this, I heard a metallic click. Evidently, the top of the pedestal was a pressure plate and lifting the vase made it trigger a latch. The entire back of the pedestal opened to reveal a safe. By this time, Green had joined me.

"Well, lookie there. That's old technology. I can crack that, no sweat."

"Seriously, Green?"

"Hey, bonus for growin' up in the hood. I'm goin' to the car. I'll be right back."

In a minute he returned with a stethoscope and a bottle of

water. He placed the bottle on top of the pedestal and put the stethoscope over the tumblers. He listened and watched the bottle. When he saw a tiny ripple in the water, he turned the dial in the opposite direction. After several ripples the safe door clicked open.

"Green, you have skills."

"I do indeed. Now let's see what we have here."

There was what I'd call a treasure map, diagramming the entire sub-basement with the location of multiple safes. Those safes, to which Green graciously applied his safe-cracking skills, held a total of five hundred million dollars. Green slipped into a cash coma. Neither of us had ever before seen so much private money in one place.

"Don't crazy wealthy people believe in banks?" Green said as he slipped back into consciousness. "There's half a billion dollars stuffed in this basement."

"Yes, they do believe in banks, but keep in mind that what's not seen isn't taxed. The Chambers family had their very own secure bank right here and had no paper trail. The government loves to tax you over and over on the same money. Madison's mom couldn't be taxed over and over on the same money if it disappeared. I don't know if we'll ever find out how she managed to do that, but off the record, I applaud her! Anyway, by the same token, none of what you see around you could be subject to estate tax when Madison's mom died. Everything was off the grid. But there must be some sort of paper trail for legitimate purchases like wine or art auction items. Sales receipts, provenances and the like."

"We'll have to see what we can find. What other papers are in the first safe that held the treasure map?"

"I've got stacks of stuff here, Green. I'll bag it and tag it as evidence and bring it back to the HUB. There's also a box of keys and some personal items. Let me remove this so that we can get out of the forensics team's way. Why don't you bag the money as evidence and I'll call a secure car to escort it back to the HUB."

"Right, Doc. Hey, can I stop at McDonald's on the way back? I'd love to pay for a Big Mac with a thousand-buck note."

"Green, you get on my last nerve."

"Yeah, I know." He smirked and walked away.

CHAPTER 13

The next morning

"**G**OOD MORNING, FBI Tri-State Task Force Director Wakefield's office. How may we help you today?"

"This is FBI Director Vale. My God, but you're extremely cheerful this morning, Ms. Henderson!"

"Well, sir, I like to project the most positive image to the public, as we are so often associated with battling the dark underbelly of society. You know, dead bodies, etcetera."

"Right. Well . . . right. May I have a word with Director Wakefield please?"

"Putting you right through, sir."

Nicky buzzed my line. "Doc, the Big Director is on line one for you."

"Thanks Nick, got it. Good morning, Keith. What can I do for you this morning?"

"Good morning, I'm going to be in your neck of the woods this afternoon around 4:00 p.m. and I'd like to get an update on the status of the Chambers investigation. I know that this is short notice, but it's a high-profile case and I'd like to stay apprised of the details and progress."

"I'm sure I can summon the troops for a briefing. I was actually about to do that anyway. Events have been unfolding rather rapidly, and we have been so involved in keeping up with our own work that none of us have had the opportunity to do much communal sharing. Perfect. We'll see you in the conference room at 4:00 then."

"Thanks, see you later."

I walked out of my office into the reception area. "Nick, would you please put the word out to the team. Director Vale wants an update on the Chambers investigation and he wants to meet in the conference room at 4:00 this afternoon. Everyone should be prepared to brief him on progress to date. Oh, and somehow diplomatically check on Green. The last time we met with the Director, he had a glob of mustard on his tie. We'd like to keep it together the best we can, ok?"

"I'm on it."

I smiled and returned to my desk. Keith Vale was not only the most capable and trusted colleague that I'd ever had the pleasure to work with, but he was also one of my best friends. We were in the same class at the FBI Academy in Quantico, Virginia, back in the day. I remember thinking how cute he was . . . tall, strong, with dark hair that was perfectly trimmed but always seemed to look a bit tousled nonetheless. His personality was the real draw. He was easy-going and funny, but also insightful and brilliant. His kind heart always shone through like a beacon.

We met on our first day at the academy. I had just gone through the cafeteria line and put my tray down on an empty table when Keith came out of nowhere. With his trademark big smile, he asked if he might sit with me. Before I could answer, he tripped, the tray went flying, and I stood covered in strawberry Greek yogurt. Without missing a beat I said, "Sure, have a seat. I'm Fiona Wakefield but everyone calls me Doc. If you're going up to grab another bowl of yogurt, could you please bring me a spoon?" Pointing at my yogurt drenched FBI t-shirt I added, "I'd hate to waste this." We both broke into hysterical laughter and his mortification melted away. He introduced himself and we started a conversation, and a friendship, that has endured for decades.

We were inseparable during our academy days. We studied together, drilled together, "hung out" with friends together, and came within inches of actually dating. As so often happens, though, life got in the way. Before we got around to becoming "an item," graduation loomed. We tied for first in our class. He was posted to Bogota and I was posted to D.C. Boom. The love story stopped before it started.

Keith was the more politically savvy and I the more psychologically analytical, so our career paths eventually diverged. Over the years, we always remained close, often consulting with one another on cases and on family. Keith eventually married but divorced three years later. I married as well and had a wonderful son. Then, three years ago, Steve died suddenly. I was shocked and concerned for my teenaged son, Chuck, who had just lost his dad . . . but my heart wasn't heavy with personal loss. I was sad but not distraught. I'd chided myself for not feeling worse. No tears. To my dismay, I actually felt a little bit relieved, as if a tense episode of life was finally over . . . and it was. Keith flew in from a conference in Dubai for the funeral. He was right there to support his godson, Chuck and me. After all, when Keith was going through the dark days of divorce, I would often call to check on him, offer support and send fresh cannolis from his favorite Italian bakery. In many ways, we were always connected.

The day blasted by and at around 3:45, the team began to gather in the conference room for the update briefing with the Director. I looked out my office window and saw three blacked-out SUVs drive into the underground parking garage. He was here. Show time. I walked into my private powder room to quickly brush my hair and check my teeth for any wayward piece of lettuce from my usual lunchtime salad. All set. I grabbed my portfolio of notes and walked down the long hall to the conference room. The team was seated around the table. After greetings I took my place at the head of the table. Director Vale stepped into the room. His entourage remained standing outside the conference room door.

"Good afternoon all, thank you for getting this briefing together for me on relatively short notice," he said with a warm smile.

"We're happy that you're able to join us and even happier to be able to share what we consider to be substantial progress in the critical first couple of days of the investigation," I said and sat down to begin the meeting.

"Atlee and Stitch, let's start with autopsy and forensics."

Atlee dimmed the lights for the slide show of autopsy photos. "Madison Chambers was a middle-aged woman in what I consider to be exemplary health. She showed no signs of disease and no defensive wounds. Madison took only vitamin and mineral supplements; she took no prescription or recreational drugs. She has had extensive plastic surgery, liposuction, Botox and Restylane injections. All were done with the highest level of care and healing was complete. That said, as you can see on slide #6, we discovered an injection site—nearly imperceptible to the naked eye—in the crease between her skull and the back of her ear."

Stitch advanced the slide to one showing a magnified image of the injection site, then the next showing Madison lying on the autopsy table, covered up to her armpits, revealing the closing stitches. She began," An advanced tox screen showed high degrees of insulin in her system. To a non-diabetic, to anyone for that matter, that amount of insulin injected would be fatal. It most certainly was the cause of death. Might I add that this was a woman who spent thousands on high-quality work and is a tribute to an organic diet and high-priced gym memberships. She cared about herself, may she rest in peace." Stitch crossed herself and sternly looked around the room until all assembled had done the same, then sat down.

For a moment there was silence as everyone stared at the slide on the screen. Then I thanked Atlee and Stitch and moved on. "Now what do you have, Detective Green?"

Green was all in green. Green suit, tie and shirt with a touch of dandruff on his shoulders. He looked like a tree that had dropped some pollen. Charming. "Well, I had the uniforms canvas the neighborhood which initially brought nothing to our attention. Then Mrs. Stein, the next-door neighbor spoke at length with Doc and me. She revealed that getting up in the middle of the night, she thought that she saw a hooded figure carrying a small white bag, like a fast food bag, walking down the side of Madison's house. The person then entered through the back door. None of the surveillance cameras near the house recorded it, but it was later found that the cameras were all offline. The tech boys are working on that as we speak.

"In any event, there is a McDonald's down the street, and we went back to interview members of the night shift who confirmed that a woman in a black hoodie bought a pancake McBreakfast that night. They pulled computer records and noted that it was a cash transaction. We're trying to track down this possible suspect. Also, while searching the house, Doc and I found the sub-basement and discovered the stolen art from the Gardner Heist along with other fine art, cash, millions in an investment wine collection, documents and keys. We are still working to unravel all of that. So far, the money is being counted and the serial numbers are being logged and checked. We've been able to verify that the wine collection was acquired legitimately. Its current value is ten million dollars."

"Yes, Doc filled me in on the details of the art theft. Frankly,

I'm stunned. We have much to follow there and I want constant updates. We still need to determine the motive for the murder. Did Ms. Chambers have any enemies? Could she have known something that endangered her?"

"We're working with Madison's family lawyer to find outlying assets. At this point the evidence seems to lead to Europe. We'll give you daily updates going forward." And looking at the entire group, I added, "I'd like daily briefings from all of you as well. The press is panting at our heels, as this is such a high-profile case. We need to make quick progress and get it wrapped up. That said, every time we do make progress, the case sprouts more legs and changes the scenery once again. Keep at it, guys. "

Director Vale chimed in, "Thanks for getting me up to speed on the Chambers matter. Before we wrap up, I'd like to briefly hear about progress in that AMC Mercedes car theft."

Stitch fairly leaped out of her seat. "My crime scene team has just finished processing the car dealership and gathering recordings from area surveillance cameras. We've also gathered traffic cam footage and I'm about to go down to the lab to sift through it all. God willing, we'll catch these dirt bags ASAP!"

"Ah yes, we all share that hope, Stitch," said Director Vale as he rose to leave. "I can't shake the feeling that this is connected to the murder."

Everyone filed out of the room, and Keith walked with me down the hall to my office. "So, it's 5:45 now. Do you have dinner plans?" he asked casually.

"Nope, just the usual leftovers sitting in the fridge."

"Ok then. Come over to my house in about an hour and we'll throw together a little barbeque. You can bring a bottle of your favorite wine and we'll hang out and catch up. If you have too much to drink or it gets too late, you can stay over. I have four guest rooms and you can have your pick."

I froze. "Is this a date? I've been a widow for three years. I don't date. I don't know how to anymore. You're a friend!"

"Whoa there, deer-in-headlights! I've seen you calmer when you're being shot at. Just because we both haven't been single at the same time for a long time, doesn't automatically make this a date. If it makes you feel better, then this is not an official date. How about I tell you when our time together transitions from casual hanging out to 'official' dating? So that said, this is just food. You still eat, don't you?"

"Yes."

"Ok, then. We're going to eat. We're going to talk. We're going to relax. Good?"

"Good."

"Now, go throw on a pair of jeans and a t-shirt, grab the wine, and I'll see you in a little bit." He smiled, patted me on the shoulder and left.

I flopped down in my chair. Was I a deer in headlights? More to the point, was this the beginning of hunting season?

CHAPTER 14

Later that evening

I DROVE UP TO the gated entrance of Keith Vale's house and greeted the suited guard who stepped out of the guardhouse with a tablet.

"Good evening. I'm 3TF Director Wakefield here to see Director Vale," I said as I flashed my badge and ID.

"Good evening, Director Wakefield. Yes, you're on my list for this evening." He picked up a red phone and said, "Agent Lewis at the front gate, Sir. Director Wakefield has arrived." The heavy, wrought-iron gates began to swing open. Surveillance cameras high in the trees were aimed at my face and car. "Please drive down to the house and park to the left of the front door. Have a pleasant evening."

"Thank you, Agent Lewis."

I drove down the long wooded road. Suddenly, like Brigadoon, the large stone mansion emerged from the evening mist. This homage to flint stone and Georgian architecture had been in Keith's family for generations. He loved it here and had spent much time and money updating it over the years. State of the art surveillance and communication equipment were necessities installed by Uncle Sam, but the chef's kitchen, indoor gym and pool were among Keith's little tweaks. His home sat on three wooded acres of manicured gardens, spacious patios and lawns.

I parked my aged but beloved Volvo and reached into the backseat for the bottle of wine that I'd bought. The front door flew open and a smiling Keith stepped out onto the doorstep sporting two red oven mitts and a barbeque apron emblazoned with the message, "Put the spatula down and step away from my grill!"

"Hey, good to see you! Come on in! The grill is hot, and I was just about to pop the turkey burgers on. You can pour the wine and shuck the corn. I've just finished making the coleslaw—I used my grandma's recipe."

"Yum. Sounds great! Let me guess—watermelon for dessert?"

"Nope. I asked my housekeeper, Mrs. Travers, to bake her famous apple pie!"

"I can't wait!

I followed Keith through the expansive living room and into a kitchen that could easily rival the professional equipment in the White House kitchen. But this one included the high-end design features of Martha Stewart's home kitchen.

"I'm guessing that you probably have a corkscrew, huh?"

"Top drawer on the left," Keith said as he took a platter of turkey burgers out onto the field stone patio. My gaze followed him outside where there was a built-in outdoor kitchen and a large teak table beautifully set with a summery tablecloth, turquoise plates, and crystal stemware. Just then, my personal cell blasted the tune "For the Love of Money," my son Chuck's ring tone.

"This is Chuck. Would you like me to put him on speaker so that you can say hi?"

"Absolutely! I'd love to chat with my godson!"

"Hi honey, I have you on speaker. I'm having a barbeque at Uncle Keith's house and he wants to say hi, too. So, what's up?"

"Hey, Chuckie! How's it goin'?" Keith chimed in.

"Hey, guys! Just checking in before the frat party starts. So, a barbeque, huh? That's your generation's code for hangin' out and hookin' up?"

"Called . . . what? Oh my god! Chuck . . . really?"

Keith and Chuck fell into peals of laughter! Then as if on cue together they said, "Gotha!"

"Ugh! You guys!"

"So, Uncle Keith, thanks for the info that you gave me on the timing belt for my car. The work I was able to do for myself saved me big bucks. I only had to bring it into the shop for some work that I just couldn't do without a lift and better tools."

I looked at him in surprise. "Keith, you don't know anything about cars."

"Yeah, but the head of the motor pool does. I included him in a golf foursome, chatted with him about Chuckie's car issues, followed up with a McCallan 18 at the nineteenth hole, and we were golden. I have a new friend, Frank, who not only plays a hell of a game on the back nine, but also volunteered to email the pertinent part of the Ford Repair Shop Manual to Chuckie, answer any questions that he had and provide a little auto shop help when necessary. It was a total win-win!"

"So, how's mom doin' with her new gig, Uncle Keith?"

"She's awesome. Just like the old days. She's back and even better than ever!" Keith said with a wink to me.

"Hellooooo—you two are talking about me and I'm here—yup, standing right here listening."

"Right Doc, be with you in a sec."

"So, Chuckie, while I have you on the phone, I need to ask you something."

"Sure."

"What would you say if I told you that I was thinking about dating your mom?"

My son answered, "I'd say it's about time! Dad's been gone for more than three years now. Mom needs to get back into life—not just work but really living. You guys have been BFFs forever—you're awesome, Uncle Keith. You should definitely take the relationship to the next level."

"Still here! Still being talked about like I'm off in Katmandu or something!" I said.

"Hang on, Mom. So, Uncle Keith, as I was saying, go for it. After all it's not like people your age have sex or anything. It's just companionship and working together to find comfortable retirement communities, right?" Chuckie was laughing so hard that he could hardly finish his sentence, and Keith was in such stitches that his eyes were tearing.

Fortunately, Chuck decided it was time to end the conversation. "Well, good talk, guys! Gotta bounce—the Friday night beer pong game is about to begin and Emily is my opponent! Love you both. Maybe *you* should play a round of beer pong too! Bye." He signed off.

"Emily? Who's Emily?"

Now Keith jumped into the conversation again. "Oh, they've been BFFs forever and Chuckie thinks it's time to take their relationship to the next level."

"Wait—how do you know all of this? You two seem like old buddies. How come you know stuff that I don't know? Oh, and don't think that I've forgotten about the dating me thing—I'll get to that later."

"Slow down. You know that Chuckie and I have always had a close relationship. After Steve died, he reached out to me a few times to talk. I just think that he needed a male role model—a guy that he knew well and could trust. Who better than his godfather? After all, he no longer had a dad to go to about guy stuff and he also doesn't have any brothers or grandpas to run things past."

"What about me?"

"Doc, you were dealing with troubles and sadness of your own. You did your best for him, but you weren't one hundred percent yet, and you were never a teenaged boy. Got to admit, I've got you beat there."

"All right, but back to this dating thing."

"Well, first I wanted to see if Chuckie was cool with it, so that his feelings were respected and that *you* knew that he was okay. Second, I want to be clear that I'm not in any way trying to replace Steve in your eyes or his. Third, we've known and cared about each other for years. Why not take our relationship to the next level? At the most, we could actually have a great time and at the least we could have companionship and a great retirement strategy. Finally, I'm a nice guy, have a good government job, am stinkin' rich and still have my own teeth. Where's the downside of giving this a shot?"

"OK."

"What?"

"I said ok."

Before I could elaborate, my purse began blasting Eric Clapton's "I Shot the Sheriff," the ring tone on my work cell.

"Saved by 70's rock." I dug for my phone, and answered, "This is Doc, what's up?"

"Doc, this is Stitch. We have a breakthrough on the stolen Mercedes McLaren case."

"What have you got?"

"The woman suspect was in a reception lounge reserved for the dealership's high-end clients. We were lucky in the sense that it wasn't regularly used and had been thoroughly cleaned the night before she was there. No one had been in there before her on the morning of the crime. We were able to pluck one hair from the chair that she sat in. It was artificial. She was wearing a wig. Just between you and me and the trees, it was a cheesy one."

"Thanks for that fashion review, but where does that leave us?"

"Well, the woman was careful, but not careful enough. She wore gloves, but she was careless in that she sipped Perrier from a Waterford tumbler while she was waiting. We got DNA and a lip print from the glass, which is just as good as a fingerprint. We ran it through IAFIS and got a hit."

"Who is it?"

"Wait, wait, there's more! I also used advanced 3D facial recognition software on the shots of her from the security cameras. It compensates for multiple factors including aging." She gasped for air, then continued. "I got a clear shot of her ear, another unique identifier like a fingerprint. Sooo there's absolutely no doubt who she is and there's a juvie file on her."

Impatiently, I said, "Stitch, who is she and is the file sealed?"

CHAPTER 15

The Following night

BACK AT THE Hub, Stitch's cell phone started to blast "Gold Dust Woman" by Fleetwood Mac—her mother's ring tone. "Hey Ma, you're calling me at work, so what's up?"

"It's nearly five on a Saturday night. You should be getting ready to go out on a date or cooking dinner for a perspective son-in-law . . . but no! You're in a lab with toxic chemicals or in a morgue with dead people. I taught you to smell like Chanel No 5, and instead you always smell like formaldehyde. How will you ever get married? You're over forty . . . you're already past your sell-by date!"

"Ma, this is our on-going discussion. You must've called me for something important, so what is it?"

"I want to talk to you in person. I'll be over in ten minutes and I'll bring dinner. I know you haven't eaten yet. Oh, and you'll invite Atlee and that nice skinny girl, Doc. I know that if you're working late, they are too. Now don't forget to tell the front gate that I'm coming. I have that special clearance now so you'll meet me in the lobby and 'claim' me from security."

"Ma . . ."

"Do not argue with me, Louisa Maria Christina. I'll be right over."

"Right. Bye."

Stitch put her head in her hands and shook it. Her mother always managed to get her crazy in a matter of minutes. Theresa Vollari was a force. To her credit, she kept the family together through thick and thin . . . and there was a lot of thick and thin in an Italian-American crime family that was slowly making the transition to "legit."

Stitch got up and walked over to Atlee's office. She popped her head in and said, "Mom's coming over in about ten minutes with some dinner—interested?"

"Are you kidding me? I don't get cooking that amazing unless I go to *my* mom's house! I'll go up and set the conference room table."

Stitch smiled, then dialed Doc's extension from the phone on the desk in the morgue. "Hey Doc, Mom's coming with some dinner. You up for it?"

"You know it! When?"

"About ten minutes. Meet us in the conference room."

"I think I have a bottle of red wine somewhere around here, I'll bring it. Bye."

The metallic orange Bentley Continental GT with vanity plates emblazoned with "MAMA" glided up to the front gate of the HUB. The driver's window slid down and Theresa Vollari reached out and handed her guest pass to the guard, her perfectly polished hot pink nails glimmering in the spotlights. She squinted at his badge and nametag. "Good evening, Agent Calloway. I'm here to visit my daughter, Dr. Vollari."

"Yes Mrs. Vollari, you're on the list. Please pull ahead to the visitors' parking area and enter the lobby through those double doors. Security will meet you and escort you from there." He picked up the phone and announced her arrival to internal security.

"Thank you. Will my car be safe here? I'm not familiar with this neighborhood."

"Quite safe, Mrs. Vollari. This is a government facility with every type of high tech protection possible. We kept the President safe when he toured a few weeks ago, so I'm sure we'll be able to keep an eye on your Bentley."

"I'm taking your word for it, young man." She pulled ahead and parked, then got out and grabbed two large picnic hampers from the backseat. She locked the car, thinking that you could never be safe enough. Upon entering the lobby, she was met by security and Stitch.

"Ciao mia bellissima figlia!" (Hello, my beautiful daughter!)

"Ciao mama! Cosi bello vederti!" (Hello, Mom. So good to see you!) They hugged and Stitch took the heavy baskets from her mom. Then she walked with her to the elevator. They went down the third-floor hallway to the conference room, Stitch clomping along in her flats and Theresa clitter-clattering along in her bright pink three-inch high Jimmy Choo stilettos. Like Stitch, she had long, dark, *big* hair and bold gold hoop earrings. Her skinny jeans fit her petite frame perfectly as did her vivid blue silk blouse. A hot orange Birkin bag casually hung from the crook of her arm. Stitch actually wore the workingwoman's version of the same outfit . . . skinny jeans, vivid blue cotton blouse topped with her lab coat and bright pink flats. She also had a bright orange Birkin bag in her office—you guessed it, a birthday gift from mom. With the two of them standing side by side, the similarities were spooky. If not for the thirty-some years between them, they could've been twins. Even their mannerisms mirrored each other.

Atlee and I were in the conference room, where we had set

up for dinner. I was pouring the wine when Stitch and her mom came in.

"Hi, Mama Vollari! Atlee and I said in unison as we went over to hug Theresa.

"So good to see you both! I'm glad that we could get together for this little impromptu dinner." Then looking at me, she said to Stitch, "La poveretta ha bisogno di un buon pasto. E'ancora solo? Posso organizzare un appuntamento con Jimmy D. Per fortuna lei non parla Italiano." (The poor thing needs a good meal. Is she still alone? I can arrange a date with Jimmy D. Luckily, she doesn't speak Italian.)

"Mama, Jimmy D. non ha collo e corre numeri per le Cavaleiros," said Stitch. (Mom, Jimmy D. has no neck and runs numbers for the Cavaleiros.)

I smiled and chimed in with, "Preferisco essere con un uomo che ha un collo e la fedina penale." (I'd rather be with a man who has a neck and no criminal record.)

Theresa's jaw dropped. Then recovering , she said, "When did you learn Italian?"

"Yesterday. I read the textbook last night. Tomorrow I'm going to learn German and I'll learn French on the plane. I'm going to Zurich next week for a case that we're working. I want to be understood in whatever language I run into."

"I forgot you just learn like that. Sorry about before, but I'm never off duty as a mom—I care about you all."

"I know, and I thank you for that. So what's on tonight's menu?"

"Vegetarian lasagna, garlic bread and antipasto."

We said grace, and all started eating. Then Mama began, "I want you all to be aware of a little family hiccup that we're experiencing. Apparently, some of Papa's business dealings from many years ago have come back to haunt him. As you know, he's phasing out his, shall we say, more risky ventures—honestly, I have never known the specifics of his businesses. He moved his headquarters to Florida years ago when he knew that Stitch wanted this type of career. He always kept her in the dark with regard to his businesses as well. He never wanted the slightest conflict of interest or trouble—even worse, he didn't want her to be embarrassed. That said, he is about to be unfortunately incarcerated for, shall we say, an accounting and income tax irregularity. He's been arrested in Florida and may be sentenced to five years in prison." Tears welled up in her eyes and Stitch put an arm around her.

"He must have a wonderful team of lawyers who will appeal the charges. How much was the apparent irregularity?" I asked.

"Two and a half million," she sobbed. Atlee choked. Then Mama added, "As you know, we travel between our homes in Florida and New Jersey but spend six months and a day in Florida for tax purposes. As I've said, his work is based down there now. We pay taxes but maybe not quite enough."

"Maybe this is not strictly his doing. Have your people look into his accountant. There may be something shady going on there. Most of the time there is more to a story than meets the eye. Unfortunately, we shouldn't get involved for obvious reasons."

"His accountant is no longer with us."

"Even though he's no longer in your employ, surely he'll confer with you," I offered.

"By no longer with us, I mean dead."

Forks fell and silence enveloped the room.

"Wait," she continued. "He died in a tragic skiing accident last winter in Aspen. My son, Vinny, was with him and told us about it. Gino, the accountant, was on a double black diamond and just skied right off the trail into a tree. The coroner's report stated that he had evidently mixed some of his medications which could cause him to become disoriented or see double.

Can you imagine such a mistake from a man whose work is so detail oriented?"

We all looked at one another and in unison said, "No!"

Then, as if the last piece of a jigsaw puzzle was put into place, realization hit Mama and her face registered sheer shock. "I have a bigger problem than I thought. The good news is that it looks like Papa may be cleared. The bad news is that it looks like Vinny has taken over the old family business."

CHAPTER 16

The Next Day

"**V**INCENT ANTHONY VOLLARI, this is your mother."

"I *know*, Ma! Am I in trouble?"

"We're going to find that out, young man! My dear friend, Sister Mary Ignatius, and I will be over in fifteen minutes. Comb your hair and shave." The phone clicked off.

Vinny felt the blood drain from his face. Not only did his mother use his full name, but she was also coming right over with the most feared woman in the world—Sister Mary Ignatius!

He thought and thought but couldn't come up with a reason why he could be in trouble *this* time. He'd been keeping a low profile lately and had even spoken to his dad about moving into the "legit" side of the family business. But there must be something that had put a huge bee in his mom's bonnet if she was bringing along her best friend, Sister Mary Ignatius. When you bring Sister along, you're bringing out the big guns! She was a human lie detector disguised as a penguin. No one could lie to her. Her dead blue eyes bore into you like a laser and then she would guilt you with doctrine until you cracked. She and Theresa Vollari had been fast friends since their grade school days at Mount Saint Mary's Academy. They'd always had each other's back.

Vinny looked out of his living room window and saw his mother's Bentley glide to a stop in front of the house. Out popped his petite mom in an orange floral silk blouse, black skinny jeans and orange stilettos. In contrast, Sister pushed her mighty, six-foot tall, two-hundred-pound frame out of the passenger seat. There she stood, on the sidewalk, a billowing black stormcloud in sensible shoes! Two of the most formidable women on earth were now heading toward his front door with the sole purpose of interrogation! Vinny began to sweat and tried to fight off an impending panic attack. He opened the front door.

"Yo, Ma!" Then noting Sister's disapproval, he amended that to, "Good morning, Mother!" And shifting his gaze added "And how are you this lovely day, Sister?"

"I walk in the light of the Lord, so every day is a lovely day, Vincent," replied Sister as she breezed past him.

"We need to talk, Vincent Anthony," said Theresa as she kissed her son on the cheek and continued into the house.

"Can I pour youze guys a stiff one? I mean you aren't strictly guys. I mean stiff tea or coffee?" Vinny was now feeling light-headed and nausea was causing him to break out in a cold sweat.

"No thank you. We want to know the details of that Aspen ski trip that you took with Gino Altieri, your dad's former accountant. You said that he had apparently mixed up his medications and that caused him to become disoriented. He skied right off the trail and into a tree. Being an accountant, he was an extremely detail-oriented person. Didn't you find it odd that he'd be careless and mix medications?" asked Theresa.

"Well yeah, but a lot was going on. His girlfriend stopped in to spend the night with him the evening before the accident and all. She's married and so the visit was on the down-low. She was in Aspen with her rich husband and he had to fly back home for business, so she wanted to spend some "quality time" with

Gino. I just saw her briefly—she didn't have much to say to me—just wanted to be alone with Gino. Hard to believe that a nerdy accountant could attract a hot cougar like her! She had a lot of influence over him—had him wrapped around her little finger. He was feeling guilty about something that she'd convinced him to do, but he never told me what it was."

Sister dug deeper, laser blue eyes on full bore. "Vincent, look me in the eye and answer the next question carefully and honestly. Did you fiddle with your father's taxes and skim off two and a half million?"

"What? No! Why would you even ask that? But wait. You think that's what this chick got Gino to do?"

"Your father is in deep legal trouble for tax evasion that he says he had no knowledge of and didn't do. He trusted Gino with his finances and taxes for years, and he's always been a stand-up guy until this woman came along. The pieces are starting to fit together. What's her name, Vincent?"

"Hcir Hctib. It sounds Middle Eastern. She's married to some rich dude. If you ask me, I think she's shady—I got a bad vibe from her."

"How long was she with Gino?" probed Theresa who was taking copious notes.

"We had neighboring condos. I saw her pull up to Gino's place around four in the afternoon. We all chatted outside for a minute—oh, come to think of it, that's probably when she left her sunglasses case on the porch—I have it here—she left before I could give it back to her. Anyway, they stayed in for dinner because I saw the truck from one of those exclusive restaurants deliver."

"Do you remember the name on the van. Do you know what time it was when they delivered?" asked Sister.

"Yeah, it was Chez Lorraine. They brought in picnic baskets and several bottles of wine around seven p.m."

"Where is that sunglasses case, Vincent?" asked Sister as she dug into the vast black hole that passed as a handbag and pulled out a pair of surgical gloves.

"Whoa, Sister, what the Hell? I mean, my goodness, surgical gloves?"

"Vincent, nuns come across lots of daily 'situations' in the course of doing God's work. These have come in handy more times than I'd like to admit." She pulled a large Zip Lock bag out of her handbag, then ordered, "Now lead me to that case, it's evidence."

Vinny led Sister into the guest room where he opened a dresser drawer. The large sunglasses case was sitting on top of a pair of ski gloves. Sister put on her gloves and slid the case into the plastic bag. They walked back into the living room to join Theresa.

"Vinny, Honey, what happened to this Hcir? Was she skiing with you boys in the morning?"

"No, Ma, she disappeared as fast as she appeared. There was no sign of her in the morning. I stopped by Gino's condo to see if they'd like to go to breakfast. He seemed sleepy and out of it when he came to the door. There were two empty bottles of wine on the coffee table. His medication was scattered all over— it looked like a bag of Skittles had exploded. Three medicine bottles were there, and the pills were all spilled and mixed up. I asked him if he was ok and he said that he'd feel better after breakfast and coffee. I told him to give a pass to skiing. He insisted that he'd be fine when he got out in the cold air. We had decided to go out to breakfast together. I went back to my condo to grab my wallet and when I came back to his condo, he was gone. He'd gone off to the slopes and had his accident. I *told* him not to ski. He could barely walk!"

"I think that the girlfriend did something with those pills. Maybe she even replaced them with something worse. Drugs can be mixed to produce a pretty lethal combination. Any way you cut it, he was toast. We need to get a look at that police report to see what kind of medications he was taking. Stitch can find that out as well as what he ingested. Meantime, Sister and I will get this case over to your sister and that nice skinny FBI girl, Doc. You've been very helpful, Honey. We have deemed you totally blameless here."

Sister nodded in agreement.

"We'll be talking to you."

Vinny saw them out, then went to the kitchen and poured himself a highball glass of Jack Daniels—it was 10:00 AM.

CHAPTER 17

I WAS IN MY office getting my briefcase packed with the documentation that I needed for my Zurich jaunt, when Nicky buzzed me.

"Doc, Stitch is here in a bit of an agitated state. She'd like to speak to you about the Chambers case right away."

"Thanks. Please send her in, Nick."

Stitch just about broke down the door as she blasted into my office. She was panting and swirling with excitement like a petite Italian twister. The only thing preventing her from breaking out and wreaking havoc was her buttoned-up lab coat which somehow seemed to contain her.

"Doc, Doc! I've connected some of our dots! The name Davinia Brockdale keeps coming up. However, the name on that juvie file that I uncovered and had unsealed was Davinia Matheson. After running the DNA and lip print from the Mercedes theft crime scene through the system and comparing it to the DNA markers in the juvie file, I got a one hundred percent match! Then, her name came up again when we digitally enhanced the McDonald's surveillance footage and got a good shot of the left ear of the person in the black hoodie who was buying the pancakes. We identified the ear using a biometric shape-finding algorithm called image ray transform. It's very much like facial recognition software. Yup, Davinia Matheson, Davinia Brockdale and hoodie woman are one and the same!"

I was about to speak when the Italian twister started to spool up and swirl again. "Wait, Wait! Just now we got a hit on the prints from that sunglasses case that Vinny said was from Gino's girlfriend, Hcir Hicib—the names don't match but the prints do. It's Davinia again!"

"Stitch, Hcir Hctib is backwards for Rich Bitch! She's playing us. This confirms what I've discovered as I've been profiling her. She's a dangerous master gamer. She amuses herself by manipulating lives." Stitch stopped dead and her jaw just dropped.

Turning to Stitch, I said, "You've done some great work here. We're finally getting a solid break in this case thanks to you. Keep me posted on anything else you find. I'm off to Zurich with Director Vale for two days of digging into finances. We're taking a government jet so we can make this trip quick and can be reached at any time. Thanks again, Stitch!"

"OMG, you are so welcome! Are you going to pick that dirt bag Davinia up?"

"I'm not going to tip our hand just yet. I'm going to put a tail on her."

"Oh, pretty slick! Well I've got to go process more items from the original crime scene. Have a good trip." She winked at me and blew out of the office.

Winked? Really? Did people think there was something up because I was heading to Zurich on a private government jet with the Director of the FBI? It's business—really!

I picked up the phone and called Detective Green. "Green, this is Doc. I need you to put a tail on Davinia Brockdale. She's a person of interest in the case."

"Okay, copy that. I'm on it."

"Thanks. Please keep me updated."

"Will do."

I finished packing my laptop and case files, grabbed my carry-on bag and headed out of the office. Nick had called for my car and driver to meet me at the lobby's front door. I was still not used to being driven around by an agent in a blacked-out SUV, but security these days demanded it.

At this time of day, our trip to the airport was relatively quick. Once there, we circled around on the inner access road until we came to the private aviation area. We drove out onto the tarmac and pulled up near the stairs of a Gulfstream G550 Jet. Another blacked-out SUV encircled by agents was already there. As we parked, the door of the other SUV opened and out stepped a smiling Keith Vale. The wind tousled his dark hair and blew open his unbuttoned black cashmere top coat, making him look a little wild—ok, wildly handsome—I'll admit it. I felt an unusual tingling. No, that's a lie. I felt as though a bolt of lightning had blown through me! I might be out of touch with my feelings, but I rummaged through the archives of my mind and dredged up the answer—I really did have the hots for him. Oh crap! This trip was supposed to stay professional. I thought, *I'll just ignore the feelings and it'll be fine.*

I stepped out of my SUV and Keith strode over to greet me. "Hey, right on time! I'm starving. I asked them to serve a simple lunch shortly after take-off. This will be a great trip. I know that we'll both gain a lot of intel."

"I'm looking forward to it. How often does anyone say that about a business trip? I'd forgotten how much I love to dig deep into a case and snap the random pieces together like Legos! Of course, the company is great too."

Keith smiled broadly at my comment.

We boarded the jet and settled into the wide tan leather seats. Our flight attendant was an armed FBI agent, as were the pilot and co-pilot. The jet was like a mini version of Air Force One. It was outfitted with advanced communication, surveillance and security systems—all tucked into a beautiful, sleek, sumptuous package. How did they do that? My musings were interrupted when a bubbling flute of champagne was handed to me.

"Oh my! Thank you so much, Agent Flores," I said as I read our flight attendant's nametag.

"You're welcome ma'am." Then she turned and handed Keith a glass.

"Thank you. You can serve lunch any time after take-off, please."

"Yes, Sir."

The flight deck door opened, and two men walked down the aisle towards us. The first one to arrive said, "Director Vale, Director Wakefield, I'm Agent McElroy, your pilot, and this is Agent Wallis, your co-pilot, for today's flight to Zurich."

"Nice to meet you, gentlemen. What does the weather look like for our trip? How long a flight are we looking at?" asked Keith.

"Smooth sailing all the way, sir. It's 12:30 now, so we'll be landing at midnight." They smiled and returned to the flight deck. Meantime, I had just snapped a photo of my champagne flute. I looked back down at my iPhone screen.

"Holy shit," I whispered to Keith. "Don't drink that!"

Before he could recover from the shock that I 'd caused, I walked down the aisle toward Agent Flores. She must've known that I'd discovered her secret, and before I could say a word, she reached for the kettle of boiling tea water in the galley. I kicked her left arm away before she could grab it and spun her around by her right arm. I wrenched it behind her back as I threw her, face down, over a seat. She started to reach for a gun with her other hand. I grabbed her wrist, lifted her up and face-slammed her into the side of the plane. She crumpled back down onto the seat and I handcuffed her. I picked up the intercom phone and told the pilot to shut down the engines and call the agency—we had an international hit woman on board.

"What the hell?" Keith exclaimed, eyes as wide as dinner plates.

"I don't know -my gut told me that 'Agent Flores' wasn't legit. I sensed nervous tension, and when she served the champagne, I observed the pulsating nerve in her neck. I snapped a picture of her fingerprint on the champagne flute and sent it to IAFIS. I got a hit. This is Angelina Torres, a Columbian national whose career choice has been a hit woman for hire since she was seventeen."

Turning to the slightly bloody Torres, I began, "Looks like you've eluded Interpol for years. Numerous U.S. agencies have a healthy interest in you as well. Now for the question that I know you've been waiting for—who paid for this hit?"

"Like I'm in the mood to 'share,'" she snarled. "You broke my nose, bitch!"

"Oh, for god's sake—I *really* hate whiners! Just shut up! Now let's put this in perspective, shall we? You *kill* people for a living and you're upset that I broke your nose? Trust me, you're lucky that you're not on your way to intensive care."

Then scrolling through the report on my phone, I added, "Okay, you've never actually been nailed before, so maybe you're not familiar with how this works. We have enough on you to put you away for the rest of your life—actually several lives. We also have extradition treaties with a number of countries where you've left quite the trail of bodies. I assure you that they aren't as humane in their questioning and treatment of contract murderers as we are. I also understand that you have two lovely children attending boarding school in England. My, my I just wonder how this will impact them? Oh, and they're minors which brings in the attractive option of landing them with social services. And did I mention that your bank accounts are frozen—even those under your aliases? Tsk, tsk, no school fees. That means they'll be out on their ears. With no other family . . . well it looks like the over-burdened British social services system does indeed get them. Too bad! Such bright futures shot down in flames."

"You can't touch my kids!"

"Oh, I think you'll find that I *can* do that and much, much more."

At this point, heavily armed FBI Agents came aboard and led Torres away. The forensics team followed and began processing the "crime scene" which was our plane.

Then turning to Keith, I said, "I'll lean heavily on her when we get back. Anyway, it'll take a couple of days to compile the volume of information streaming in on her. She'll likely never see the light of day again. Playing the 'kid card' is the key to breaking her. In the meantime, looks like we'll need another plane. We're already running behind schedule."

Keith smiled. "I've already taken care of it. Here comes our ride now." Looking out of the window I saw another Gulfstream taxi up next to us on the runway. Nice to have a few connections, I thought.

Our pilot and co-pilot, Keith and I walked over and boarded the other jet as our luggage was transferred. Local FBI agency chief Don Wallace greeted us on board and verified that the plane was totally secure down to the last toothpick. "I don't know how Torres slipped through. She is an uncanny dead ringer for the real Agent Flores, whose body was just found in a dumpster at the end of the runway. We'll back-trace security, credentials, travel routes—everything. This is personal now. Torres has killed one of our own. Thank you, Director Wakefield, you prevented the situation from escalating."

I nodded. Then turning to Keith, I added, "I think I'll take over the flight attendant duties for this trip. I've had enough drama for one day and I'd like to relax and process."

"Absolutely," he smiled. Then to Agent Wallace he said, "Get me some answers! I'm pissed about what happened here today. Tighten up security! Now let's get the hell out of here. We have a lot of work ahead of us."

With that, Wallace left, the plane hatch closed, engines revved, and we began to taxi down the runway.

After take-off, I went to the galley, poured two glasses of champagne and put some cheese and crackers on a plate. I popped the pre-made meals into the microwave to warm. I brought our "cocktail hour" goodies to the table on a tray and sat down with Keith. He smiled at me and his eyes actually twinkled. "You never cease to amaze me. You literally saved our lives—and the lives of the pilot and co-pilot. You know that they would've been disposed of as well—collateral damage. Your instincts always seem to be engaged on high alert—always have been as long as I've known you."

"It's just the way I'm wired. I'm looking forward to finding out where these pieces lead. I can't help but think that this little episode is somehow related to our current case. I can't shake the feeling. Anyway, let's take a break and have cocktail hour and something to eat."

We nibbled cheese and crackers like companionable little mice and sipped champagne—then sipped more as we chatted and ate our shrimp scampi. We began to set up our respective game plans for the next day. Keith was going over notes and files in preparation for the meeting with his Swiss counterpart, Federal Councillor, Guy Parmelin, head of the Federal Department of Defense, Civil Protection and Sport. The Federal Intelligence Service was under his umbrella. In the meantime, I spread my files all over the leather couch and began to see whether I could "Lego snap" some of the informational pieces together before I met with officials of Credit Suisse the next day. I also had a folder of documents and a handful of keys that I assumed went to safe deposit boxes. I had to get to the bottom of that "Aladdin's Cave" in our victim Madison's basement. I knew that she was no criminal mastermind, though she was complicit in the cover-up. It was her mom, Frances Ogden Chambers, who was knowledgeable in fine art, wine and apparently, high value crime.

Time passed and I looked out the plane window. I saw a bright moonlit night. Suddenly feeling sleepy, I put my files away, kicked off my shoes and lay down to take a nap on the couch. Just as I was falling asleep, I felt Keith tuck a throw over me and gently kiss my head. He was pretty special.

"Hey Doc, wake up and smell the coffee! We'll be landing in Zurich in about an hour. I've made some eggs and toast to go along with that coffee."

"Yumm, thanks! Let me go splash some water in my face and I'll be right with you." The bathroom was pretty spacious for a plane, with plenty of counter space and a lighted makeup mirror. After freshening up, I joined Keith for breakfast.

"We'll have two cars meet us at the airport. You'll be headed to Credit Suisse on the other side of Zurich, and I'll be headed to Bern about an hour and a half away. Let's meet at Clouds around seven for drinks and dinner. Aside from the wonderful food, it has the most breathtaking views of the city at night. Then we can haul ourselves back to the airport and head home.

"That sounds fabulous! Something wonderful to look forward to after a long and jet-lagged day."

We finished our breakfast and prepared for landing. Once on the tarmac in Zurich, I walked down the steps of the plane and got into the Mercedes- Maybach S600 that awaited me. Keith got into its twin parked right behind mine. Nothing like traveling in style. A bit nicer than my eleven-year-old Volvo with the broken gas gauge and shopping cart dings on the doors.

The Credit Suisse offices at Paradeplatz 8 were every bit as upscale as the clients who frequented them. The building was in the classic old world European style that put me in mind of England's Selfridges Department Store. Despite the artisan craftsmanship and genteel aura of a bygone time, make no mistake that the most advanced technology and security systems lived within.

A concierge greeted me, and I was escorted upstairs to the private banking suite. I was transferred to the care of a very gracious, beautifully dressed woman named Mrs. Huber, who seated me in a sumptuous, light-filled room and offered me tea. Ten minutes later, she led me to the office of Mr. Fredericks, the head of the private banking division.

"Ah, Dr. Wakefield, it is my pleasure to meet you. I have all of the legal forms and documents in order and I have been in contact with Mrs. Chamber's personal attorney. I trust that all is in order and that I can shed some light on this situation."

"I appreciate that, Mr. Fredericks. I've brought some documents and keys that I found in our investigation of the Chambers' home. I hope that you can shed some light on their meaning as well."

Mr. Fredericks reached over and took the items that I offered him. He took a moment to read the documents and examine the keys. "Well, Dr. Wakefield, this certainly answers any questions I may have had and fills in the final pieces of the puzzle for me. Let me tell you what we have here. This is quite a family saga that was buried for decades and was only to be revealed upon the death of Mrs. Chambers and her daughter Madison."

My ears pricked up like a German Shepherd's, and I found myself sitting on the edge of my comfy leather chair. "Please do go on, Mr. Fredericks."

"First of all, we do have a numbered bank account containing sixty million American dollars belonging to the late Mrs. Chambers. The documentation that you provided shows that the numbers correctly match our account records. These keys are the depositor's set of keys that go to four safe deposit boxes. Three are Chambers family boxes and one, on which there is a restriction, is a Missy Matheson box. I was only to allow the Matheson box to be opened under two circumstances. One, if foul play was suspected in the death of a family member and it was being investigated by governmental agencies. This is our current situation. Or two, when the late Mrs. Matheson's estate was finally settled. I believe that's two years following her death. Actually, that date should be coming up shortly. We can go to our vault in a few moments and open them together. All of these assets can be released now that the formal paperwork is filed." He rose and walked to a side door in his office. "Please follow me."

We walked down an emerald green-carpeted hallway to an enormous armored vault door. Mr. Fredericks asked me to turn as he punched in the pass code followed by a retina scan. The door unlatched and automatically opened, revealing an ornate room filled with safe deposit boxes of varying sizes. In the center of the room was a large, beautifully carved antique mahogany table with a thick green felt top. Mr. Fredericks accompanied me to four separate boxes. We pulled each out and placed them all on the table.

Opening them was quite the revelation! The first box contained the documentation for the wine collection. This was assembled over the course of about ten years, and the receipts were meticulously catalogued. The wine was obtained from auctions and private sales worldwide. The wine collection was strictly legit. Next was a box containing, literally, the family jewels. Velvet boxes from Harry Winston, Van Cleef

& Arpels and Cartier were among many others containing rings, pendants, earrings and bracelets of flawless emeralds, diamonds, sapphires, rubies and a mélange of other rare gems. I examined the settings and stones with a jeweler's loop and noted that most of the collection's pieces were antique, dating from the nineteenth century. There were some classic pieces from the early twentieth century as well. I was stunned by the exquisite craftsmanship and absolute beauty of these one of a kind pieces. There were bills of sale from jewelers and auction houses and a few handwritten "provenances" from family ancestors. Again, no anomalies—these were legitimately purchased by and inherited through the family.

Now to box number three ... documentation of another kind ... and a bit darker this time. There were carbon copies of letters and notations of phone conversations between Frances Ogden Chambers, Madison's mom, and Timmy O'Leary, a legendary high-end thief. My heart started to pound as I read on. These contacts were, indeed, made in 1990. At the time, Mr. O'Leary was a key player in the Irish criminal world of Boston. Was he actually a member of the Irish mob? Unclear. It really didn't matter—he certainly was deeply connected to the dark underbelly of serious crime in the area. I turned the page, and there it was! The actual "contract" put out on specific pieces of art at the Gardner Museum. Frances Ogden Chambers paid Timmy O'Leary the tidy sum of two million dollars for the "transaction," with the caveat that no one was to be physically harmed in the process of the "acquisition." There was also the promise of a one-way first-class plane ticket to the Maldives, which to this day has no U.S. Extradition Treaty. With that amount of money, O'Leary could live out his days like a king. In fact, there have been no "sightings" of him since the heist—he essentially fell off the radar.

I had to sit down. This revelation was almost too much

for me to take in. Here, in my hands was the solution to the largest art theft in history! Proof positive that demure socialite and philanthropist, Frances Ogden Chambers, was a criminal mastermind. Who knew?

I had to calm my racing mind, as there was one more box to open. The Missy Matheson box. Though the family was shattered, Missy was the custodian of the family history. I lifted the lid and found stacks of legal documents and handwritten notes. Upon examination, I realized that I was looking at a complex family puzzle, the likes of which I could never have imagined!

This was like a breadcrumb trail through the family. We began with the marriage license of Frances Ogden Chambers and William Cummings Matheson in 1959. Included were pictures of the event as well as the full-page New York Times account of the wedding which appeared in their society section. Like a royal wedding, this was clearly the joining of two obscenely wealthy and powerful dynasties. They moved in the highest social circles worldwide. Bride and groom both had Ivy League educations to supplement their already established pedigrees. The groom was working for the family financial firm and the bride was to lead a family philanthropic organization. They were the perfect couple.

Next came yet another revelation—birth certificates—yes, plural! It was commonly known that Madison Chambers was an only child. Here was her original certificate, showing the birth date of June 9, 1962 and her original birth name of Matheson. But wait, there was another birth certificate with the same date! Davinia Matheson must have been Madison's twin! But wait again, a *third* birth certificate listing another girl, Parker Matheson! Triplets!! What the hell happened to this family? I told myself to focus and press on, as this was the mother lode of family secrets.

Digging into the next document in the pile, I came to the Matheson's divorce decree dated in 1963. It came about back in the day when there was no such thing as a prenuptial agreement, even among the wealthiest of families. This document stated that Frances kept all her family financial holdings and half of their marital assets. The same arrangement applied to William. What came next was rather stunning, especially for the times. Frances went back to her maiden name and retained full custody of Madison, whose last name was legally changed from Matheson to Chambers. William got sole custody of Davinia Matheson, and the third daughter was privately adopted! Who would do such a thing and why? As I read on, the situation became clearer. These families were two warring empires. There was clearly no love lost between them, and for a while at least, Frances and William were exactly like Romeo and Juliet. Soon, the beautifully poetic forbidden love sank into an alcohol-fueled and adulterous tsunami and was totally destroyed. How tragic. According to some tear-stained personal family letters in the safety deposit box, both families took a hard stand and the children were like the sacrificial lambs in this divorce drama. Each warring faction insisted that there be no interaction of parents in the raising of the two girls. They were never to know of their other parent or sisters. The third daughter, Parker Matheson, was to be eradicated from the family knowledge all together, and placed with a well-off and highly-educated family. She, being the third of the three born, was seen as an unnecessary "overage" and was just not wanted.

There was one shining star in all of this. Missy Matheson, William's mother, was the only grandparent—actually the only family member—to care about little Parker. It occurred to me that it was time to search through all of Grandma Matheson's papers and track down her beloved grandchild. I needed to find out more about the Mathesons. I believed this had a bearing on Madison's murder. As a matter of fact, Grandma Matheson, Margaret "Missy" Matheson, had passed away about two years before. I remembered reading her impressive obituary in the New York Times. By all accounts, she was indeed a good woman . . . and an old one . . . as she checked out of "hotel life" at one hundred and one years old. She apparently led a full life until the end, then simply faded away in her sleep. Her many philanthropic causes were her legacy. I made a note to contact the Matheson's lawyer for the rest of the family information.

I gathered all of the documents together, and placed them in my briefcase. Mr. Fredericks gave me the contents, then replaced the four boxes and walked me back to his private reception area. We said our goodbyes and Mrs. Huber escorted me down to my waiting car. I asked my driver to take me to Clouds, where Keith and I had agreed to meet for drinks and dinner. I texted him in case he was still meeting with his Swiss counterpart, Guy Parmelin. Seconds later he called me. "Hey there, I'm done with my meeting and am on my way to Clouds. I should be there in about twenty minutes, what's your ETA?"

"I'll be arriving at about the same time. Could we take a few hours off and just relax? Maybe enjoy dinner and chat like the old friends we are? Save the shop talk for the plane ride home?"

"Absolutely! In fact, I was going to suggest the same thing. We've been running around like a couple of hamsters on a wheel and it's now officially down time. See you in a few."

I smiled as I hung up. What a nice guy he was. I really looked forward to our "date," short lived as it would be, since we had to be back at the airport by 11:00 PM. Well, at least we had carved out some time to get back in touch on a personal level, which was no small task for folks in our line of work—especially since we often work together. I looked out the car window as we maneuvered through traffic and finally pulled up to the restaurant. There was Keith, standing on the sidewalk, waiting for me. He smiled like he had when I met him for the first time years ago. He opened my door and kissed me on the cheek, then took my hand as we walked in together. "Hey Doc, you look great even after a long day!"

I beamed at him. "You have no idea how nice it is to hear some kind words at the end of the work day. I can get so caught up in the intensity of the work, that I forget I have a human side too. Thank you."

"I've reserved a table with a view and the wine is chilling, so let's relax for a couple of hours. We can debrief later on the flight home."

"This is a date then?"

"Yes . . . *Finally!*"

Despite the traditional exterior, the restaurant's interior was sleek and modern with a distinct upscale, sophisticated vibe. It had the look of an exclusive hang out for rich and famous foodies on the Upper East Side of New York or Downtown LA. The modern art on the walls, the cool jazz playing in the background and the chic couples sipping cocktails, had the most delicious calming effect on me. As we were seated at our table, Keith looked at me and nodded knowingly. "Well, this has had the desired effect on you! I can actually see you soaking in the atmosphere like a sponge. I thought that you might enjoy it here. It came highly recommended, and the food is supposedly amazing."

"I *love* it! This sounds a little crazy, but I feel tapped back into my real self, sort of my old self, if that makes sense."

"It does. I know that you're the psychologist and the expert, but sometimes you forget to care for the essential *you*. That's when a simple hunch by an old friend who knows you pretty darn well can make a little difference. I'm glad that your 'Zen' is coming back and that my hunch was right."

I felt an incredible warmth radiate from the center of my

chest all the way out to the tips of my fingers and toes. This man was truly kind. He was special to me, and now I not only knew it, but I felt it too. I smiled and was about to speak when our waiter appeared with chilled wine and menus. He greeted us, poured our wine and mentioned the featured items. Then he withdrew to give us a moment to make our selections.

"I'm going with the steak. The shallot and mushroom glaze sounds perfect."

"I have to say the salmon with the lemon-dill butter has my vote." As if summoned by telepathy, our waiter magically reappeared to take our orders.

We dined and chatted, laughed and sipped wine . . . and thoroughly enjoyed ourselves. The food was fabulous and the evening came to an end way too soon. Duty called. It was time to make our way back to the airport.

We exited the restaurant and were standing on the curb waiting for our car to come. For some reason, the hair on the back of my neck prickled up. I glanced down and saw a red laser dot on my chest. Instantly, I dove to the sidewalk, dragging Keith down with me. The shot blew past us and destroyed the door of the restaurant behind us. Bystanders began screaming as Keith grabbed his phone and called for help. I looked up and saw a black helicopter with no tail number lift off from the roof of the building across the street. Gone.

"Are you ok?" Keith gasped as he came to help me up.

"Yeah. Just some scrapes . . . you?"

"Fine. Did you see anything other than the chopper?"

"No, but they were clearly targeting only me."

Police and agents swarmed the area. Emergency vehicles with red and blue lights flashing and sirens blaring blocked the surrounding streets. Miraculously, no one was hurt. The sniper left no trace behind. The police reported that there were no shell casings in the sniper's nest on the rooftop across the street and the surfaces were wiped clean—with Clorox. Another pro!

We answered questions and finally got into the car to head to the airport about two hours later. We called ahead to have the plane completely searched and an extra security detail put in place in preparation for our arrival. We also had a police escort to the airport.

Once on the plane, I kicked off my shoes and poured each of us a large whiskey. I flopped down in the chair and buckled up for take-off. Keith did the same, then stared at me and said, "So who the hell is after you and why? I just got the summary of the "flight attendant" hit woman's interrogation back in Newark. They aren't done with her yet, but apparently she was contracted to kill you and decided to make me collateral damage in order to muddy the investigation. She figured that the agency would assume that I was the target and the focus would be on me. When they came up dry on that, they'd begin the investigation on you, thus buying her a bit more time to get out of the country."

"The only thing I can think of is that the threads all seem to lead back to one woman with several aliases and a recently unsealed juvie file. There are wealthy families involved, so you can imagine the roadblocks that have been put up, the high-powered lawyers that are on retainer and the money that's involved. The good news is that I must be right, and I must be close or there wouldn't be a hit out on me."

"You call that the *good* news?"

CHAPTER 18

Hours later

I WAS SO WIRED from the excitement that I threw myself into fleshing out and finishing the profile on Davinia. What a dark and twisted narcissist she was. Totally pathological and extremely dangerous. I was so absorbed and lost in the work that I wasn't even aware of the time passing.

We landed back in Newark where a blacked-out SUV was waiting for us on the tarmac. Keith and I exited the plane while our luggage was removed and transferred to the car. We were both exhausted, so we fell into quiet companionship on our ride back to the HUB. He dropped me off, giving me a warm smile, and a kiss on the cheek while another agent brought my bag upstairs. I wearily wandered to my office, took a shower, changed my clothes and laid down on the couch in my office for an hour's nap.

Slightly refreshed, I made a cup of coffee and sat down to call Clive Hunter, Missy Matheson's attorney. "Good afternoon, Mr. Hunter. This is Tri-State Task Force Director Wakefield calling with regard to a case we're currently investigating."

"How can I be of assistance to you today, Director?"

"I'm investigating the murder of Madison Chambers. In the course of my inquiries, I've discovered that she was a triplet, raised by her mother following her parent's divorce. Her sister, Davinia, was raised by her father, and her other sister, Parker, was privately adopted. It was decided that the girls would know nothing about each other. Their paternal grandmother, Missy Matheson, was the only family member to follow the lives of all three girls."

"This is highly confidential information that has been carefully hidden for years. May I ask how you discovered these details?"

"The details impact my case. Suffice it to say that I've been through the family's safe deposit boxes in Zurich."

"I see. Well then, yes, Mrs. Matheson was a warm and loving woman She had great love and pity for her abandoned granddaughter and didn't want to lose track of her. Detailed adoption information and the subsequent name change were known only to her, and were documented in her private papers, which I have here. They remain sealed. She also set up a massive trust for the girl in her will. Parker is her only heir. According to the will, I am to unseal that information and disperse the inheritance exactly two years after Mrs. Matheson's death. As you may know, that will be in a few weeks. Anyway, she retained a private investigator to keep tabs on Parker, follow her and keep an ongoing photo record of her life."

My heart grew warm as I thought of this woman who was forced to keep her distance from a loved one, but nonetheless would not relinquish that love. She was the only one who cared enough to really "know" Parker (or whatever her adoptive name was now) and yet Parker to this day, was to have no knowledge of her.

"Mr. Hunter, what are the particulars of Mrs. Matheson's will?"

"Neither Madison nor Davinia were to benefit from her will unless Parker pre-deceased them, in which case they would inherit her entire estate. There's something interesting of late. As our clients are in a way connected, Madison's attorney contacted me last month, regarding a recently made codicil to her will. Apparently, Davinia found out about Madison, contacted her and began to bond with her. You may not know it but Davinia is the rather evil black sheep of the family. She somehow convinced Madison to make her the beneficiary of the will. Madison had no other heirs and was apparently so thrilled to have a sister that she willingly agreed. Davinia was supposed to return the favor and put Madison in her will, but I have no knowledge of that being done.

The little-known twist that Madison secretly added to her codicil was that the inheritance would revert to her grandmother's trust account, which she knew remained open, if her death was due to foul play. I now wonder if Davinia could have found out about that account and told Madison? At any rate, she knew that the account was set up to distribute the money wisely even though she was not privy to the details. Apparently, the New York Time's extensive obituary on Missy Matheson made a vague mention of a link to the Chambers family as well as the many charitable organizations that Missy supported. Perhaps one or both girls had seen it. One doesn't know how some of these closely guarded family secrets sometimes leak out."

"I don't yet know how it could have happened, but I have a strong hunch that Davinia might know about the existence of their third sister too. If so, this could be extremely serious and dangerous to that sister. Please contact me if Davinia contacts you."

"I certainly will. It's been a pleasure speaking with you today, Director."

"And with you as well, Mr. Hunter. You've been a wealth of knowledge. Many thanks. Goodbye."

Now my blood ran cold. This black sheep was out to make

a killing—literally. The evidence was pointing to Davinia, and now I had the motive. As usual, she needed to advance her evil game, but there was also a huge inheritance in play. It was time to interview her. Green and his guys had her under surveillance, so I gave him a call.

"Detective Green, this is Doc. Please meet me at the HUB tomorrow morning at nine. We're going to pay Davinia Brockdale a call and interview her."

"About time. She's a squirrely chick! Rich as all get-out. Married to a dude who pretty much owns Wall Street and just quietly reads for fun. She's always drinking by the pool, throwing parties and drinking with friends, running poker tournaments and drinking with her poker buddies, drinking and racing vintage sports cars around her estate. In her spare time, she's just drinking."

"Charming. Well let's see if we can catch her in a rare sober moment. See you in the morning."

"Yup."

Jet lag was finally catching up with me. I picked up the phone and dialed my assistant's extension. "Nick, I'm going home now to crash, so would you have them bring the car around please?"

"On it. Have a nice night."

After a good night's sleep, in the morning I felt more human. I put on a nicely tailored navy blue pants suit, with a crisp white shirt and heels. I looked a little too stiff, so I added a pretty Hermes silk scarf that I had gotten for a good price at a local consignment shop. Now I struck that professional-yet-chic note that I was striving for!

My car and driver picked me up at eight o'clock and we proceeded to the HUB. I had some time to complete a bit of preliminary paperwork. Then at nine o'clock sharp Detective Green arrived. We got in the car and headed out west on New Jersey route seventy-eight to horse and estate country. After about half an hour, we pulled up to the Brockdale's estate. We showed our IDs to the guard at the gate who phoned the house to announce us. The high gates swung open, and we were directed to drive down the long road to the yet unseen house and park on the right side of the circular drive. We did, and were then met at the front door by a man in a crisp Italian suit, who looked as if he hadn't smiled since the Carter Administration.

"Good day. I am Jeeves, the Brockdale's butler."

"You're kiddin', right? Jeeves, the butler? Really?" Green snickered until I sharply nudged him in the side.

"I'm Tri-State Task Force Director Dr. Fiona Wakefield and this is my colleague, Detective Green. We're here to speak with Mrs. Brockdale."

"You don't have an appointment, so you'll have to wait a few moments for Mrs. Brockdale to become available. Please follow me."

He led us through a palatial front hall, through the living room, and out French doors to the pool and patio area. We were seated at a lovely table with an umbrella and offered coffee, which we gladly accepted. We were soaking up the atmosphere when an impeccably well-dressed man with an expensive briefcase walked over to us. He was handsome, with strong features and graying temples. I detected sadness about him.

"Good morning. Isn't this the most beautiful day? I'm Robert Brockdale. I understand that you're here to speak with my wife."

"Very nice to meet you, Mr. Brockdale. I'm Director Wakefield and this is Detective Green of the Tri-State Task Force," I said as I shook his hand. Green did the same.

Mr. Brockdale smiled. "Well, I must say that your very impressive reputation precedes you, Director."

"Thank you so much. Yes, we're here to discuss several matters with Mrs. Brockdale."

"Well, I'm sure she'll be with you in just a few moments. Will you excuse me? I'm expected at a virtual meeting shortly. It still amazes me that I can conduct business wirelessly in the back seat of a car on my way to the office. It was nice to meet you both. Enjoy this glorious day!" He shook our hands and walked briskly out to his waiting town car.

"Nice guy," said Green with a slight air of surprise.

We sat and sat and sat for about another half an hour, when finally, we heard the click of heels echoing in the hallway. Out onto the patio stepped a perfectly groomed Davinia Brockdale, wearing white slacks, a simple black tee shirt and large Jackie Onassis-style sunglasses. Her heavy gold hoop earrings, diamond encrusted Rolex and three-karat engagement ring spoke volumes about her wealth. However, something about her instantly made the hair on the back of my neck stand up and I got a strange feeling in the pit of my stomach. These were red flag alerts that I'd always gotten around the worst of people.

"Good morning, I'm Davinia Brockdale. Jeeves informed me that you'd like to have a word. May I ask what this is in reference to?"

"Yes, Mrs. Brockdale. It's nice to meet you. I'm Director Wakefield and this is Detective Green. We're with the Tri-State Task Force, and our questions are in regard to a series of events linked to the murder of Ms. Madison Chambers."

"That's been all over the news day and night. How could I possibly be of assistance? I didn't know Ms. Chambers."

"Where were you four nights ago? Sunday night."

"Surely you don't think that I had anything to do with her death! I was here at home all evening."

"Can anyone vouch for that?"

"Yes. My husband was here as well . . . somewhere. Oh, I'm sure he was reading as usual and I was doing the final planning for a party that we're hosting here this coming weekend."

"We'll need to speak with him later. But at the moment, we

have evidence that places you at several crime scenes, and we need to take you in for further questioning."

"Wait! You can't do that! My lawyers will have me out by noon! I'm no felon!"

"Oh, I think you'll find that you actually are, Mrs. Brockdale! You'll need that lawyer," said Green as he rose and put handcuffs on her.

"Jeeves, call my lawyer! *Now!*" screeched Davinia as we marched her outside and put her in the back of our SUV.

As we passed Jeeves, I heard him say under his breath, "Nasty bitch is *finally* getting what she deserves!"

Wow. There's trouble in paradise. My guess is that Jeeves was in no rush to call that lawyer! I walked back over to him and said, "We will send a detective from our team out later to ask you a few questions and take a statement."

"My pleasure to assist, Director."

So off we went back to the HUB to interrogate Davinia. She looked absolutely shocked to be in custody. I had been assembling her extensive profile. Tying together the threads from her juvie file, her family history and her actions of late created a chilling scenario. She was a dangerous narcissist and a true sociopath. The psych evaluation in her file said that she had these tendencies, but they had become fully developed as she matured. Manipulation was her strong suit. She was a nice-looking woman who used looks, money, influence and charm to get whatever she wanted—always. She had succeeded so deftly to this point, that she was convinced of her own infallibility—almost super human in her ability to do anything that she pleased and get away with it. She had no regard for the lives of others. To her, robbery, embezzlement, manipulation . . . even murder were just part of a game. It was as if everyone was a pawn on a giant chessboard, and she was the omnipotent grand master directing all the moves. It was just for her amusement.

After all, she didn't *need* anything. She had money, influence, mansions, cars, designer clothes, a private jet . . . you name it. Her motive had nothing to do with any of that. It was all about her ability to run a flawless game for her own twisted enjoyment. She did things because she could. This is the most dangerous of criminal minds because it's all about the narcissist. There's no respect for human life and not a shred of compassion or remorse—ever. It's absolutely chilling.

Back at the HUB, Davinia was placed in an interrogation room where Green began with some preliminary questioning. I scooped up his case files as well as my own and headed to the conference room for the meeting I'd called.

As I passed her desk, Nicky grabbed me. "Doc, Mr. Hunter, the attorney for Missy Matheson's estate called. His secretary has disappeared. The Matheson file, containing the specifics of the will and the information about Parker was found unsealed and on his file vault floor. He has no idea how long it's been there, as it's a seldom used storage area."

"Oh God! That's most likely Davinia's doing. If so, she knows all about the third sister. Send a couple of detectives and a forensic team over to that office right away!"

I hustled over to the conference room. "I apologize for being a few minutes late. We've just brought Davinia Brockdale in for questioning. Detective Green is beginning the interrogation as we speak. Let's snap all these pieces together if we can. If my hunch is correct, we have a master of murder and deception downstairs. Let's go around the table and see what we've got. Atlee, you're on."

"Okay. As we said, Madison Chambers was in perfect health. She was given a lethal injection of insulin behind her ear—right in the crease where the ear meets the skull. It was nearly imperceptible. We later found that her empty coffee cup revealed traces of Rohypnol that showed up in huge amounts on her advanced toxicology screen. Essentially Madison was 'roofied,' you know, the date rape drug. It isn't hard to get hold of, can be administered in a drink and will turn the victim into a rag doll within twenty minutes. There were no signs of a struggle, so Madison knew her attacker. The crime scene was also staged. How do I know, you ask? Well, it was at first a hunch because Madison was dressed for a meeting and her breakfast was on the table. Yet her time of death was around three in the morning. So how many people are ready for work then?

We discovered that the home surveillance system was' frozen' by a portable jammer, so only neighbor Mrs. Stein saw a hooded figure enter the house. However, Madison, for some reason, had her cell phone on a table and the video was on. Unbeknownst to the intruder, the murder was recorded. The hooded figure was Davinia. She entered the house, they hugged, she handed Madison a cup of McDonald's coffee, and they sat in the living room to chat. Apparently, Davinia was in a faux crisis about her marriage and needed her newly found sister's shoulder to cry on. Once Madison passed out from the drugged coffee, Davinia injected her, changed her clothes and propped her up at the kitchen table. As we verified with ear recognition, it was Davinia buying the pancake breakfast at McDonald's. She just set it up like a breakfast scene on TV."

"What was her motive?" asked Atlee.

"Davinia preyed on Madison because it thrilled her. She found out that Madison was her long-lost sister and conned her into making her the beneficiary of her will, since Madison had no other family."

"What about all of the stuff in the sub-basement of the house? The Gardner Heist?"

"To our knowledge, Davinia didn't know about that. She was quick but not thorough. The Gardner collection has been verified and returned to the museum with their unending thanks. The fabulous wine collection is legit and we have the documentation for that. It's part of the estate and for now, is in evidence, as is the money that we discovered down there. The documents and keys that Green and I also discovered in the safes led us to the Credit Suisse Bank in Zurich. I'll get to that in a minute. For now, let's move on. Thanks for your findings, Atlee. Now Stitch, what do you have?"

Stitch stood and began, "It was our friend Davinia who pulled off the Mercedes robbery as well. Her lip print and DNA were found on the glass at the dealership. She forgot about that. She was getting sloppy. Though she wore a wig, theatrical makeup and gloves as a disguise, she drank from a Waterford glass in the customer waiting room. As with the surveillance cameras at the house, the traffic cams near the dealership were "frozen" by a magnetic jammer that we found on the car. Our folks had been watching the ports and picked up the Mercedes as it was being off-loaded from a tractor-trailer truck on the docks at Port Elizabeth. It was about to be loaded into a container headed for Dubai. Her 'associates' spilled their guts to save their own skin and lighten their sentences."

"Stitch was the one who discovered that Davinia also had a sealed juvie file and pushed legal to get it unsealed."

"Yup," Stitch beamed.

"Oh, and Stitch's mom, Mrs. Vollari and her friend Sister Mary Ignatius opened up another line of inquiry. Stitch, why don't you catch the group up on the ski accident and your brother's involvement while I shoot a quick text to Detective Green and see how he's progressing."

Stitch recounted the Aspen story and how her dad's unfortunate accountant, who was her brother Vinny's friend, had died. The sunglasses case left behind by the accountant's married girlfriend, Hcir Hchtib, was absent-mindedly picked up by Vinny who gave it to his mom and the sister when they questioned him. They brought it to Stitch for processing.

Stitch continued. "As you can imagine, this was no innocent skiing accident. I ran the prints from the sunglasses case and it was Davinia again. As Doc pointed out, Hcir Hctib is Rich Bitch backwards—she was just playing her game. We had enough evidence to have Gino's body exhumed, God rest his soul. Reports showed traces of alcohol and his prescribed diabetes medication in his blood. We looked harder and found healthy traces of Rohypnol. He was 'roofied' too. It had dire results, as he went 'rag doll,' then skied right off of the trail and into a tree. When she no longer needed Gino for her game, Davinia got rid of him. We also had a forensic accountant go over Gino's books to determine whether he was intentionally harming my dad. He did, in fact, embezzle millions from dad and put it in an offshore account—the pin was given to his 'girlfriend.' More importantly, he told my dad that his taxes were paid and filed but they were not. A trail of deleted emails shows that this was also done through manipulation by his girlfriend Hcir Hctib who, as I've said is Davinia. It landed my father in jail for a crime that he didn't commit. She simply wanted to mess up lives just because she could. A prominent Italian-American 'business family' was a perfect target. The prosecutors now have all of this information, and the charges against my dad have been dropped."

Everyone at the conference room table clapped. Stitch broke down in tears, and then slowly composed herself. "Mama is so grateful to us all. She's planning a thank-you dinner."

"Thanks, Stitch."

"I'd like to jump in here, if I might," added Keith. His face displayed a darkness that I seldom saw, but which I knew to be a sign of pent-up rage.

"Absolutely."

"As you know, the other day, Doc and I had a quick there-and-back Zurich trip to follow various leads associated with the Chambers case. While traveling, there were not one but two assassination attempts on Doc's life. At first, we thought that I was the target, but evidence now points to Doc. When my team is put in danger, I take it personally and will not rest until those responsible are incarcerated. I am incensed! I consider it to be my personal responsibility to ensure the safely of all of you. That said, here's what we now know. The hit woman who posed as an FBI agent/flight attendant is a career killer wanted internationally. She's a single mom, and we used the future of her kids to leverage information from her. She's also never been arrested, and through her disillusionment, weakened and finally cracked. She was hired anonymously through emails. A shell company paid her. We kept back tracing this shell company until we came to the end of the trail. We realized that it was a nearly forgotten entity owned by a Brockdale subsidiary. The emails were traced back to a server at that company. When our people raided the building, it was an empty warehouse with a laptop. Guess whose fingerprints were on the laptop keys?'

"Oh no! But why would Davinia want to kill *me*? I only just met her this morning. I've never had any dealings with her," I said as I began to sweat.

"Well, wait a minute, there's more. The puppet master deepened her game. When she found out that the hit in Newark was thwarted, she was pissed and had to quickly find another way to get the job done. She got sloppy again. She called in a favor of an old employee who 'owed her.' Dieter Klaus had once been a soldier-of-fortune type and family bodyguard to the Brockdales. He exited their employ under unfortunate circumstances. Apparently, he was caught pilfering some of Davinia's jewels to finance a little gun-running side hustle that he had. She caught him and let him go with the caveat that he owed her. She knew that his type could come in handy someday. So, she covered with a story that Dieter was just a petty thief who needed to be fired and forgotten. She never pressed charges. She knew he'd returned to his native Zurich, and so she contacted him to contract the hit. She arranged to provide him with the gun, chopper, and identifying information. She had a private detective in Zurich follow Doc to take photos and get the details of where she was having dinner. There was plenty of time to arrange the hit while Doc and I worked, then had dinner. Our people, working with INTERPOL picked Dieter up at the helipad when the chopper landed. He hates Davinia so he spilled the whole story. He actually admitted to intentionally fudging the shot so that no one would be injured. The only thing that we can't figure out is motive."

I was still a bit startled, but I tossed in my two cents. "I've profiled Davinia, a copy of which you'll find in the briefing packet that I just passed out. As I've mentioned before, she's a dangerous narcissist, a sociopath. It very well may be that she tried to kill me because she thought she could. Just a challenge in her twisted mind. I got a very disturbing, deeply angry vibe from her when we met this morning. She can't deal with failure. She feels that she should be able to manipulate her pawns flawlessly to achieve her desired outcomes. Having me there at her house this morning was almost more than she could bear. Her anxiety levels were through the roof. She was sweating, fidgety, and unfocused. After all, I'm supposed to be dead and yet there I was, a testament to the failure of the latest moves in her game."

"Green didn't get anything out of her and she's lawyered up," said District Attorney Andrew McCallister. He continued. "We are arresting her and charging her on multiple counts. We have two counts of murder, grand theft auto, attempted murder and conspiracy to commit murder, and financial theft . . . so far. I'm asking the judge to deny bail, as she's a huge flight risk. I'm also not planning to put any deals on the table. But maybe in our discussions I can find out a motive for the attempts on your life, Doc."

"Do you think that they'll go for an insanity plea?" asked Keith.

"If I were her lawyer, that's what I'd do," said Andrew.

"If she's as in love with herself and as detached as I think she is, I don't see her going for it. As a matter of fact, I wouldn't be surprised if she fires her high-priced attorney and represents herself," I offered.

"Holy shit, what a nut case that Brockdale woman is!" said Stew Green who had just joined the group. He leaned against the back wall by the conference room door and added, "Her husband just arrived and doesn't seem concerned about this whole situation. I don't think it's denial, I just think that she's worn the poor guy down."

"Oh, there's more news," I added. "Just before the meeting began, Nicky reported that Mr. Hunter, Missy Matheson's lawyer called. His secretary has disappeared and the sealed family file was found opened and on the floor of a seldom used file vault. I've sent detectives and forensics over there. I'll bet that Davinia is behind this and that she knows the identity of the third sister."

"Folks, thank you for all your hard work. This is coming together very well and in record time," remarked Keith.

I left the conference room and went to the ladies' room in my office to splash some cold water on my face. I can usually hold it together and remain detached, but having a nut job put hits out on me was disturbing to say the least.

"Hey, you okay?" asked Keith as he popped his head into my office.

"Yeah, just a little shaken."

"Would you care to accompany me to a quaint bistro for a light dinner and a couple of glasses of fine wine?"

"Indeed, I would! Can you give me about an hour? I need to have a few words with Mr. Brockdale and freshen up a bit."

"Sure. That will give me a chance to visit the crime lab and speak with a couple of the folks down there. How 'bout I meet you back here in an hour then?"

"Perfect."

Keith left and I went down to have a chat with Mr. Brockdale. It was true; he was beaten down by many years of dealing with his wife. He was fed up with her constant drinking and partying, her disregard for any other human being on the planet, and her disdain for him. He was only there out of obligation. Clearly, he was a good guy, and had no idea that Davinia's dark hobby was to ruin the lives of others. He was genuinely shocked and deeply dismayed by that. He'd taken her to the best psychiatrists over the years, only to have her make excuses to leave their care. He and Davinia had finally drifted into separate lives and barely interacted at all anymore.

I wrapped up the interview with this poor man whose wife had just been arrested, arraigned, and was being transported to prison to await trial. An orange jumpsuit was a far cry from her extensive designer wardrobe. And not for nothin', orange was *not* her color!

Keith and I got a quiet table in the enclosed outdoor garden of a quaint little restaurant near the HUB. It was nice to breathe for a moment with someone whose company I thoroughly enjoyed and with whom I could just relax.

"You look really lovely tonight, Doc."

"Well, you're so kind to say that!" I actually felt myself blush as I reached for my glass of wine.

"We should do this more often. I think the recent events have made me realize how precious a relationship we have. I'd love to spend more time with you."

"Well, I think that you're right."

"Now at the risk of you getting that deer-in-the-headlights look again, how about we drive out and spend next weekend at my house in the Hamptons? Before you say anything, I do have six bedrooms there, so we can just go without awkward expectations if that makes you feel more comfortable."

Before I could answer, the waiter came to take our orders and after discussing entrees we went off topic and on to another conversation. We had a lovely dinner and Keith dropped me off at my house, as we both had hectic days ahead. Oh, and just so that you know, I texted him that the Hamptons weekend was a great idea. And no, you don't get to find out any other details!

CHAPTER 19

NEARLY A MONTH had passed since we'd brought Davinia in. As I had anticipated, she had fired her legal team and against their advice, had decided to represent herself. Her trial was set to begin in the morning. I decided to visit her in prison the day before. She apparently planned to continue her game. Davinia now acted deeply self-assured, smug, focused and flippant, all signs that she was getting the game back on track and most probably planning to inflict harm. I was a thorn in her paw, an annoying challenge, so she hated me.

"How are you, Davinia?"

"I'm better than ever, thank you, Doctor. I'm more than prepared for my trial tomorrow. Those fools on the jury will love me and wonder why they're even wasting time with a trial when I get done with them. You look well," she sneered. "I'm planning a special surprise for you. It's not ready quite yet. Still in the contemplation stage I'm afraid. But no fear, it'll be ready soon. I can hardly wait to see the look on your face when you receive it." She was seething with such extreme anger and I detected a slight tremor in her hands.

"How very thoughtful. I'll see you in court tomorrow."

Davinia shot back, "I'm smart and capable and will represent myself brilliantly."

"Good luck with that." I turned and left. I just needed to quickly assess her one more time in order to confirm my final profile. As I had anticipated, it was chillingly accurate. Davinia's mental illness, coupled with her present situation, had heightened her frustration. In turn, that had made her seethe with anger and amp up her desire to inflict harm. The target could be anyone, but I just seemed to be the current annoyance. My heart pounded and I decided to put a special security detail on myself. I knew that even from behind bars, this woman was a threat. No one was off limits. Anyone could be a pawn in her game.

The next morning was bright and beautiful. I hated to spend it captive in a courthouse. I chose a nicely tailored black suit and a teal silk blouse for the occasion. I arrived at the courthouse and sat on a bench in the hallway outside the courtroom. Keith showed up first, followed by the rest of the Task Force Team. We were all being called to testify. Mr. Brockdale paced at the end of the hallway. Poor man. He really was a nice person. Tragically, he had married an evil woman. I'm sure that she presented herself as a different person when they first met. I'm also sure that her charm was her key point of manipulation, as she deftly maneuvered him into marrying her.

Brockdale was unhappy in the marriage, but never knew the full extent of her mental instability and evil until recently. He seemed very beaten down and frankly, ashamed of her. He went into the men's room—I absent-mindedly thought that he had just enough time to go before court began. Looking out of the window, I saw the prison van pull into the downstairs courtyard. Out stepped Davinia, perfectly coiffed and wearing a pink and black Chanel suit. The shackles were nice fashion accessories!

I could hear the elevator stop, and Davinia stepped out. Suddenly, Mr. Brockdale hurried over to her, and yelled, "You won't ruin any more lives!" He shot Davinia point blank in the forehead! As quickly as I'd ever seen anyone move, he spun around to me, and before anyone could subdue him shouted, "You're the third triplet, Parker! You're now free and so am I." With that, he shot himself in the head.

Stunned the assembled crowd seemed to move in slow motion. Both Davinia and her husband were pronounced dead at the scene. I felt my whole body go numb and I fainted dead away.

When I awoke, I was on a gurney with an EMT taking my vital signs.

"How are you feeling, ma'am? Your vitals are fine now. You were lucky. From all accounts when you fell, you just crumpled, and Mr. Vail caught you before you hit your head on the floor."

"I'm okay. Just feeling a little weak and shaken. Could I have a bottle of water please?"

"Yes ma'am, here ya go."

I thanked him and went over to sit on the hallway bench. Keith looked dazed. The coroner and forensics team had arrived. The area was corded off and the bodies were being readied for removal as the crime scene was being processed.

Keith gave me the information about what had happened. "Brockdale got the gun from the men's room. It was hidden behind the HVAC vent. Someone on the inside must've put it there for him. He never could've gotten a gun through that metal detector down in security. When the shock of the shooting dissipates, you'll be able to relax in the knowledge that your life is no longer in danger."

"I'm the third triplet? I can't believe it. We need to get a DNA sample from Davinia and Madison and compare them to me. I mean, I knew I was adopted. I had the most adoring adoptive family, but I would never have imagined any of this."

"I'm bringing you over to my house today. I'll ask Nicky to go over to your place and grab some clothes. You'll need a few days off while we sort this all out."

"I don't have the strength to argue."

I went over to Keith's, curled up on the couch in the den and fell sound asleep. Hours later he sat on the couch next to me and gently woke me up. "Well, Brockdale paid a janitor to hide the gun in the men's room. I also found out Davinia paid off the lawyer's secretary to access your grandmother's file. We followed the money trail and found her on a beach in Mexico. She's being extradited as we speak."

"This is the day that the attorney is supposed to deal with Missy Matheson's will. Finally, my dear, you *are* Parker Matheson. Your adoption papers held by your grandmother's attorney verified that. I just got off the phone with him. We also ran your DNA against Madison's and Davinia's—you are definitely all three triplets. I'm so sorry that you were the one put up for adoption. What a convoluted family secret."

"Oh, don't feel sorry for me. Out of the three of us, I was the one who had the most loving upbringing and turned out the best. I only regret that I never knew my grandmother. She was the only family member who really loved me."

"And she really did! According to her confidential papers held by the attorney, she attended every one of your graduations. In fact, after you received you doctorate from Harvard, she donated a huge amount of money to your department. Ever hear of the Matheson Chair in Psychology?"

"Yes!"

"She was also at your wedding. She sat in the back on the groom's side so that she wouldn't be noticed. She was at the hospital when Chuck was born, and at the back of the church, once again, when he was christened. She was at his graduation from high school. She was at your graduation from the FBI Academy. There's a file of pictures taken at every milestone in your life. She hired a private detective to follow you all the time. She wanted to know all about you and made sure that you were safe. She was, in fact, your guardian angel. She loved you very much. You were her favorite."

I began to sob. "This woman loved me unconditionally all of my life and I never knew her. I only wish that I'd met her."

"Apparently you did. Think back a bit now. Do you remember an elderly lady speaking to you after your Harvard graduation? She was a trustee and she approached you to congratulate you. She had a quiet manner and a habit of holding a person's hands in both of hers as she spoke."

"I *do* remember that! At the time I thought it odd that a trustee who was a total stranger showed me such warmth and sincerity."

"As only a grandmother could! It was the only time that she was able to touch you and speak to you. It was the highlight of her life."

"Oh my God!"

"Now you are the sole heir to the Chambers/Matheson fortune. Mr. Brockdale amended his will a couple of weeks ago. Yes, you're the beneficiary of that as well. He wrote that he admired your integrity, intelligence and tenacity to find the truth. It's clear that you were part of the plan when he decided on this murder-suicide. I would imagine that, given all this information, you are easily one of the wealthiest women in the world."

My jaw just dropped as I struggled to take this all in. I felt such love for the grandmother who had loved me throughout my life. How I wish I'd known the woman who'd guarded me from afar for all of those years. How I wished that I could always feel the warmth that I'd felt during that brief graduation handshake. I told Keith, "The money doesn't mean anything. I wish that I'd known my grandmother."

"She left a letter for you. Here, read it."

Keith produced a large manila envelope that had been couriered over from the attorney's office during the afternoon. I opened it and read the letter. Tears streamed down my cheeks as I absorbed the words of a sincere and loving woman. She was kept from me by legal parameters and the mores of a lost time. Her love beamed through and I felt the warmth of her words as I read them. A red velvet box was also in the deep envelope. It contained my grandmother's golden locket. When opened, it revealed a picture of me on one side and a picture of her and my dad on the other. This would become my most cherished possession. I wear it always.

The sun was setting now and dinnertime was approaching. Keith's housekeeper, Mrs. Travers, came in to tell us that she would be serving in about ten minutes. "I put an extra bottle of wine out to help you both relax and absorb the events of the day." She smiled warmly—a very motherly smile from a wonderful woman who was like family to Keith.

"Thanks, Mrs. T." he replied.

"Doc, honey, how are you doing?"

"I honestly don't know yet, Mrs. T. There's so much to take in."

She came over and wrapped me in a huge hug. "You are a triplet, a beloved granddaughter, an heiress, and you were saved by an unknown brother-in-law. That *is* quite a lot to take in!"

Keith continued, "Davinia put those hits out on you. She needed to get rid of you just as she needed to get rid of Madison in order to win her game and inherit the entire Chambers/ Matheson fortune. She likely wouldn't have stopped trying to have you killed, even from behind bars. My guess is that eventually she would have eliminated her husband as well. She wanted to inherit his fortune too. He learned what she knew and what she was up to, so decided to put an end to her and her personal brand of evil. She had ruined his life and left him an empty shell of a man. He must've felt that he had nothing to lose anymore, so devised a murder-suicide plan. He saved you."

Mrs. T. was simply stunned. "This is an unbelievable maze of events. How long ago did you discover all your family secrets, dear?"

"The pieces didn't snap together until today, Mrs. T. You see before today. . . ."

Keith blurted, "She never knew."

I felt like I'd been dropped into the vortex of a tornado. I couldn't figure out how to wrap my head around this. I'd gotten up and started my day just as I'd started any other day. But today wasn't any other day. Today I found out that I was the unwanted child of two warring dynasties. That when my parent's marriage ended and everything was split equitably, I couldn't be split so I was 'donated', much as the unwanted clothes that I'd collected for my church. The shining star in this tangled tale was my grandmother, Missy Matheson. Though I never knew her, she certainly knew and *loved* me. Now I truly loved her as well.

Family drama aside, I'm now an heiress. Not just a minor heiress mind you, but a mega heiress, if there is such a thing! Will this change me? Yes, because now I'm pretty sure that I can pay off my son's student loans *and* my mortgage! I'm not going to get crazy and buy a new car. Mine has a few good years left. I'm not going to trade in Keith either. I figure that he has a few good years left too. I'd like to spend those years together.

ABOUT THE AUTHOR

Deb Nicholson is a life coach and CEO of Recipe 4 Life Coaching, LLC. Her love of writing began in elementary school when she won the award for "Best Creative Writer" in her school district and was honored by the Superintendent of Schools. Pretty heady stuff for a fifth grader! Since then, there has been a book bouncing around in her head, and it finally found its way to the printed page.

Combining her self-professed mystery addiction with encouragement from the local writers group (FAWG) and inspiration from the Malice Domestic Conference, Deb has concocted her first cozy mystery.

In her spare time, Deb likes to meditate, travel, run, visit museums . . . and contemplate her next book!